The Secret
Forbidden Amish Love Book 3
Tattie Maggard

PLEASE NOTE: This is a Swiss Amish series (not Pennsylvania Dutch) consisting of three parts: The Broken, The Forbidden, and The Secret. They must be read in order.

4.92 ≠

Chapter 1

Another summer had come and gone, and the September breeze felt crisp and clean. Emily waited on the porch with Silas for his children to arrive. This was no usual visit, however. Natasha had failed a grade and wasn't fitting in well with her new peer group, causing even more problems in school. Her *mueter* had decided to let her live with Silas for a while, hoping she would get caught up in her studies under the strict eye of the Amish school teacher. Will, not wanting to be left out, was following along.

Emily hoped the new arrangement would keep Silas busy and allow him time to bond with his children. She also hoped she could handle the two *Englisher* students in her classroom.

Silas tapped his foot anxiously on the porch step.

"Can I get you some sweet tea while you wait?" Emily asked, looking down at his foot.

"No, thank you." He self-consciously stopped the bouncing foot and shifted his weight.

Her eyes narrowed on him. "Are you nervous about the children coming?"

He hesitated, stroking his beard. "A little."

Silas seemed to tell Emily everything, and she wondered what had been on his mind he hadn't shared since Jada first informed him of the big change.

"Everything will work out in God's will; you'll see."

Silas smiled, holding her gaze for a moment. It wasn't a drawing pull, like the many moments they had shared together on the porch before, but one of mutual admiration.

Just then, Jada's car rolled up the drive, sending Silas to his feet and out to greet them. Emily watched from the swing as bags were unloaded from the car and carried inside. Jada was thin as a rail, with exotic-looking black hair halfway down her back.

A strange thought popped into Emily's head. *They'd both kissed the same man.* An uncomfortable feeling crept over Emily, and she tried to think of something else, hoping the awkwardness wouldn't translate to the relationship with her new students.

Supper was served in Silas's kitchen, and as Emily turned to go, Natasha asked, "Where are you going, Miss Emily?"

Flustered, Emily replied, "I think I'll go home a while and get some mending done before school in the morning."

"Did you already eat?" Will asked.

"Nay." Emily shook her head.

Silas motioned for her to sit. "It's all right, Emily, if you'd like to eat with us tonight. You did make all the food."

"All right. I'll be back with my plate." It would be nice to eat with Silas and the children, rather than in her kitchen alone, but she wouldn't have dreamed of it without Silas's permission, and she couldn't be making a habit of it. Silas was very clear about the way they must conduct themselves going forward.

At the table, Silas said grace, then he began

4

telling the children how things would be a little different for them at their new school.

"Does the school have electricity?" Will asked.

"No. No one around here has electricity, not even the school." His voice was soft with the children, making Emily admire him even more.

"Well, how do they charge the computers then?" His forehead was scrunched tight.

"They don't have computers."

"Or smart boards?" Natasha asked.

"They have no electronics and neither will either of you. This will be different than when you two stay the weekend. You'll be learning things that you wouldn't at your old school and I want you to dress like all the other kids, and try to get along with everyone. Do you understand?"

They nodded their agreement. "Who will my teacher be?" Natasha asked.

"I will," Emily chimed in.

Natasha's face brightened.

"Who's going to be my teacher?" Will asked.

"I will," Emily said again, watching the boy's stunned reaction.

"How can we have the same teacher? I'm in the third grade and Natasha's in fourth."

Silas's eyes glistened. "She teaches all the grades."

"Wow," the boy said, and Emily laughed. She hoped he was half as impressed after a full day of school with her.

Emily spent much of her school day evaluating Silas's children. Will was a bright boy of ten, with a sharp mind for mathematics. He was very disappointed to find that not only did the school not have computers, but that he wouldn't have a science class, his strength at his former school. Emily set him to work with an arithmetic book and sat Natasha in a chair beside Emily's desk.

"All right. Read this to me." Emily handed the girl a reader she would expect a girl of her age to use.

Natasha shook her head, her dark hair flowing over her shoulders. Emily had started a dress for her but hadn't finished it yet. The girl wore a pink sundress with short sleeves, and a picture of a cartoon unicorn on the front, stamped in glitter. "I can't read that. It's for adults to read. I need a kids book."

Emily pressed her lips together. If she wanted a kids book, she'd give her the simplest one she had, forcing the girl to request a harder one on her own. Letting the girl see for herself what level she was would build confidence. But when Emily handed her the primer and the girl stumbled over small words like in, is, and was, she immediately saw there was a big problem. "Okay, Natasha, that's enough." She took the book from her and set it down.

"I want you to write a sentence on this board, about anything you want." She handed the girl a small, white, dry-erase board with a black marker and pretended to busy herself with the papers on her desk while she waited. After several minutes, Natasha handed her the board. Most of the words were spelled incorrectly, some not even phonetically, and her handwriting was atrocious. "Thank you, dear," Emily said calmly.

"Now I want to know how well you know your arithmetic facts." Emily set a page in front of the girl with one hundred simple math facts in all four operations: addition, subtraction, multiplication, and division. "Work as quickly as you can, but try to get the right answers. It's okay if you don't finish, but I want to know how many you can do in three minutes."

The girl nodded and started in. Just as Emily feared, at the end of three minutes, Natasha had only finished a few problems correctly and her sevens were all printed backward.

"You knew she was dyslexic?" Emily couldn't believe what she was hearing. Why hadn't Silas told her this in the first place? At least she could have prepared herself. She stood with Silas between the two houses on the dirt path that connected their kitchen doors.

"The school told us last year when she was about to flunk. When the evaluation came back they decided she was dyslexic, and because it was a learning disability they passed her on and let her take all her tests orally, with no time limits."

Emily's mouth dropped open. "The child can't read or write," she whispered.

"And that's why she's here. I told Jada you could do a much better job than any of those teachers, and we couldn't just sit around waiting for her to get more behind each year."

Emily couldn't decide if she should take that as a compliment to her teaching abilities or if she'd been bamboozled. How was she to give Natasha the extra help she needed to catch up to her peers and be a teacher to the rest of the students? "She's testing at three years behind, Silas. I've had students like this in the past, but never this far behind."

"I believe God has put you in her life for a reason. You're a good teacher, Emily. Just do your best."

Emily let out an exasperated breath. It was good to know Silas wasn't expecting a miracle. At this rate, just getting her to a second-grade reading level would be a challenge. She looked up at him, catching a glimpse of a smile. She narrowed her eyes. Did he think this was funny?

He whispered, "Has anyone ever told you you're pretty when you're overwhelmed?" Silas was giving her that look. The one he always got a few days before telling her they should keep their distance. Emily crossed her arms in front of her. He would be of no help today. She shook her head at him tightly, and turning on her heel, marched back to her kitchen, slamming the door behind her.

"Is this a 'b' or a 'd'?" Natasha asked a few days later as she pointed to the word, pushing the book in Emily's face.

With flour on her hands, Emily squinted to see the shaky book in the girl's hand. "B." Emily went back to kneading the dough as the girl read some more.

"Tr-tribe?"

"Very *guete*. Keep going."

A moment later, Natasha asked again, "Is this a 'b' or a 'd'?"

"Okay, honey, set the book down and come help me." *One step at a time.*

Natasha did as she was told, setting the book on Emily's table and coming back to the counter.

"This dough will be the biscuits for tonight's supper. I want you to roll them all out and shape them into 'b' shapes. Make a dozen of them. Do you know how many a dozen is?"

"Twelve?"

"That's right. Make twelve 'b's and lay them on this baking sheet for me, okay?" Emily got out a pen and wrote the letter 'b' on an index card and taped it to the counter, leaving no room for mistakes. If she hadn't, she feared Natasha would move the card and start making 'p's or 'd's or even 'q's. "I'll be back in a few minutes to see how you're doing."

Emily slipped outside and met Silas and Will coming from the henhouse. Will handed the egg-basket to Emily, one egg cracked and leaking.

"Danki," she said wide-eyed, trying to smile.

Silas nodded to Will in dismissal and watched him run off behind Silas's house. Emily hadn't spoken to Silas in days and was beginning to crave an apology—or any interaction whatsoever. Natasha was taking up every moment of her day, it seemed, inside the school and out.

He glanced her up and down. Then he said, "I'm sorry about the other day."

Emily didn't want him feeling bad on her account. She whispered, "It's okay, Silas, sometimes I get the urge to kiss you, too." She lifted one corner of her mouth.

He laughed as she turned and went inside. She enjoyed teasing Silas, as long as it didn't get out of hand. Neither one of them were considered young anymore and it was nice to feel desirable, even if it could never be acted upon.

Back in the kitchen, Natasha had six 'b's on the baking sheet.

"*Guete* job. Keep them all the same size and they'll all get done baking at the same time."

The next day, when Natasha was reading aloud to Emily in the classroom, she asked, "Miss Emily, is this a 'b' or a 'd'?"

"What kind of biscuits did we have for supper last night?"

"B biscuits? Hey, biscuit starts with 'b'."

"That's right. Now, do you remember what the 'b' biscuits looked like?"

"Yeah, I have a picture of them in my mind."

"And the next time you come across a 'b' or a 'd' and you wonder, you can pull out the picture of the 'b' biscuit and know what a 'b' looks like. If it's not a 'b', it must be a 'd', right?"

The girl's face lit up. "That's really clever, Miss Emily."

"*Danki*. Now keep reading. You've still got five pages to go." Emily's little trick worked, but judging by Natasha's handwriting she'd need to relearn all the other letters in the alphabet as well. Emily listened to Natasha read as she formed a plan for supper.

Suddenly, Will was standing beside Emily's desk, "Why does she get to sit up here and talk to you all day and I have to do these worksheets?"

"She has her assignments and you have yours. Have you finished?"

"No."

"Then get back to your seat until you've finished."

He went, but not without hesitation and a stern look from his teacher, a strong indication he was going to be trouble.

Each time biscuits were called for in a meal, Emily would have Natasha make a set of twenty-six, one for each letter of the alphabet. Sometimes it would be the lower-case alphabet, and sometimes the uppercase. When she got really good, Emily would have her start her cursive letters. In addition to that, Emily would quiz Natasha on her arithmetic facts as they prepared meals. "If I chop this carrot into twenty-four pieces and give you half, how many pieces would I have left?" Emily asked, one evening before Jada was to pick them up.

"Twelve?" Natasha wore a pair of pants with a long-sleeve shirt. Silas had told her to leave her plain dress at home for her visit. Emily was planning to surprise her with another if she could make time over the weekend. "That's right. Don't forget any of your arithmetic facts while you're gone."

"I won't, Miss Emily. I'm going to make biscuits for my mom."

"Would you like me to write it down for you, how to make them?"

"No, thanks. I've got it all right here." She pointed to her head.

"All right. Well, let me know how they turn out when you return on Sunday evening."

Emily chopped more carrots while Natasha cut up some potatoes, throwing them in a large pot as they worked. When the stew was finally on the stove, the sound of Jada's car door sent Natasha running for Silas's house.

A few minutes later, Silas was at the door. He didn't knock, but she preferred it that way. Still, it was odd for him to visit like this.

"You must be feeling mighty strong today," she said teasingly.

It took him a second to realize what she meant, but when he did, he reached for the door knob.

"It's okay, Silas. I think we can have supper together without incident, don't you?" She smiled at him knowingly.

"It's different having the kids here, isn't it?" he said, sitting down.

"*Ja,* they keep us busy."

"And accountable," Silas added. "It's nice to be able to eat with you at the table again."

"I know what you mean. Without the children present, I probably wouldn't see you much at all until spring." Could it be they had found something that worked for them?

"How's Natasha coming along with reading?"

"It's not just a reading problem. It extends to her writing and math, and everything she tries to do. But I'm seeing improvement. It's just going to take time."

"Well, I never dreamed I'd see her dressing plain and making biscuits, that's for sure."

Emily laughed. "I'm going to make her a new dress this weekend if I have the time."

"Thank you."

"Well, every girl needs more than one dress."

"I meant for everything. I know this can't be easy for you. I've caused you a lot more work and I know my kids have a long way to go at learning the ways of the people."

"You're welcome, Silas." She stared at him a moment, admiringly. Emily was finding it very rewarding to teach Natasha. Perhaps God meant her to have a family after all.

Chapter 2

Emily peered over her shoulder at Natasha as they worked in the flower garden. The little girl of eleven was now a blossoming young woman of fourteen. It was difficult for Emily to push away pride when the last few years came to mind. When Natasha came, she could barely read or write, but now, with considerable work and attention, she was one of Emily's top students. But school was out for the summer and Emily feared what would happen next. Silas had been hinting for a while now about Natasha going back to live with her *mueter*.

"Do you think we could make some of that fancy lemonade to go with tonight's supper?" Natasha asked. The girl had become quite good in the kitchen and must enjoy working there because she was always requesting "fancy" things to be made for ordinary mealtimes. She really had fun when special occasions came around.

"If you want to make it, go right ahead." Fancy lemonade was tinged pink with berries. Emily loved having Natasha around. Not only was the work of keeping up with two houses getting done, but they were together constantly, talking and laughing. Emily had even taught Natasha to yodel when they worked, breaking out in a song when they ran out of things to say.

"I made the chocolate lava cake for Mom over the weekend."

"And she ate it?" Emily nearly dropped her hand rake.

"No, but she tried a bite."

"Well, that's pretty big for Jada." It had finally stopped being awkward to speak of Silas's ex-wife in conversation. Emily had let go of the negative feelings she had for her soon after Natasha came to stay with Silas. "How is she getting along with your *step-vater*?"

"Pretty good. I hope she stays with this one. I told her she needed to settle down before she gets too old."

Emily laughed. Natasha did too, once she saw Emily laughing.

"How old is she?" Emily asked. She tried to remember if she'd ever heard anyone say.

"Thirty-seven. She's two years older than Dad."

Emily was twenty-nine, younger than both of them. She thought back to when they first came to live beside her. Faintly, she remembered Silas with a short beard and Jada, large and round with child, but Emily had only been fifteen at the time, and not the least bit interested in who was moving in next door. Now Emily was an old maid, but with Natasha to help pass the time, Emily didn't seem to mind.

"Well," Natasha said, standing to look at her work, "that's that." It was her saying when she'd finished with anything. "I'm off to start supper." And with a dusting of her hands, she was on her way to Emily's kitchen. The girl could make supper all by herself if she wanted, but Emily stood as well, to go help.

From the side of the house, Silas came around

16

without Will. Any time Emily and Silas crossed paths without the children near they would stop for a word or two before going on their way. It was the only time they had to talk to each other until the every-other-weekend visits with Jada left them home alone again.

"You look handsome today. Going somewhere?" she asked quietly, always conscious of who might overhear. He had his black felt hat on and trousers with no suspenders—his town clothes.

"I've already been."

"You've been to town already? I had no idea you were gone." It wasn't like Silas to leave the place without telling her. She wondered if he'd told the children.

"Jada and I needed to talk about the kids."

"What's wrong?"

"We've decided it's time for them to go back and live with Jada."

Emily raised her hands up to her mouth. "*Nay,* Natasha loves it here."

"We want them both to graduate high school."

"What for?" Natasha had just finished her last year at the Amish school and Will only had one year left.

"Because they may not always want to be Amish and we feel their education is important."

It was a slap in the face. Emily's hands fell at her sides, her fists clenched. "You're sending her back to the same school system that said she was learning disabled and would need someone to read her tests for

17

her because you feel education is important?"

"I knew you wouldn't take this well."

"Silas, she's a good girl, but she's becoming a woman. If you send her back into the world now, you could lose her. If she stays, she could join church in a few years, settle down and marry a nice Amish boy." She was trying to put ideas in his head, ideas he should have been thinking on all along.

"She wants to be a school teacher, like you."

Was there hurt in his eyes?

"What's wrong with that?"

"I just want what's best for my little girl, and I think she should go to college and get all the education she can."

The *Englisher* ways ran deep. At least in Silas they did. He had all the indications of his mind being set: clenched jaw, the two marks on either side of his eyebrows and eyes firm, where usually they were so playful when she and Silas were alone.

"What do you think Natasha is going to say about it?" she asked.

"I don't think she's going to like it. Which is why I'm telling you first."

Emily shook her head. He wasn't going to get her help on this one.

"I want you to help me convince her it's best for her to go back."

"I won't do it. If she wants to stay, you should let her. I want no part in this." Emily hoped something would be said or done to stop this. Natasha was like a daughter to her. The daughter she would never have, otherwise.

"She can stay the rest of the summer if she wants, but she starts high school in August."

Emily turned away from Silas, heading across the backyard, to the mimosa tree they planted a few years ago. There she sat and cried for what Natasha would face in the *Englisher* world. Then she cried for herself, feeling like the old, lonely spinster she was.

Silas wondered about Emily. Each time they crossed paths in the yard she had puffy, red eyes from crying. It made him wonder if he should re-think his decision to send the kids back to Jada. He loved having them there and hoped one day they might join the Amish community, but Will was ready to go back and he worried Natasha would only want to stay until it was too late to finish her education. He couldn't let her wait until she was twenty to decide to finish high school and go to college. As parents, they had to be realistic. And that was the problem. Emily had become too attached. She wasn't Natasha's mother—but she wanted to be.

Silas walked into the barn and picked up the small wood-carving he'd ruined, wondering where he'd gone wrong. He'd tried to make a heart-shaped wooden box with a lid out of the old mimosa stump for Emily but had failed miserably twice now. Figuring a heart was too fancy for an Amish woman anyway, he decided to try again with a simple circle. He hoped it would work out, and that Emily would one day forgive him for taking Natasha away.

Everywhere Emily went she saw people with
their young children, hugging them, dragging them
along by their hands. It seemed every woman had a
baby in the crook of their arm or jumping up and down
on their lap, and Emily was starting to feel almost
conspicuous without one. What did the people think
when they saw her out at her age with no child at all in
her arms or at home waiting for her?

Tears came quick and often, and Emily
struggled to know why. She had been so happy before,
but now what? She hated to think that Silas might have
been right, that she would regret her decision not to
marry, and refused to tell him what was really on her
heart.

It was almost Christmas when he came into her
kitchen and sat down at the table. He'd been allowing
them to eat their meals together even though the
children had left in August. Emily figured it was
because he was trying to cheer her up, and so she
determined never to cheer. First, she liked having Silas
in her kitchen again, and second, she still hadn't figured
out why, after all these years, she suddenly had a baby-
shaped hole in her heart.

She poured a cup of coffee and set it in front of
Silas. He hadn't taken his coat off yet, so she figured he
wasn't planning on staying long.

"May I take your coat?" she asked. It wasn't
something she normally did, but she longed for him to
stay and not leave her alone with her thoughts this

dreary day.

He gazed at her tenderly, and with some hesitation, he gave the coat up to her, but not before pulling something out of the pocket. Emily hung the coat by the kitchen door and sat down beside him, scooting her chair a little closer.

"I'm sorry this took so long." He handed her a white, paper-covered bundle, not much bigger than the palm of his hand.

A present? Maybe she could allow herself to be cheered for a moment. Opening it, she saw a wooden box, hand-carved, with a lid that opened and shut with tiny hinges. "It's beautiful," she said, nearly in tears already. It was a thoughtful gift, something much too personal for ordinary friends to share.

"It's from the mimosa—your mimosa, the one that I had to cut down."

She studied the box. "You made this for me out of my tree?" Tears were forming, blurring her sight.

"Yeah. I hope you like it."

Her chin shook. Flashes of her brothers and sisters came to mind, the mimosa's pink puffs giving off a fragrant perfume in the warm air. They'd fanned themselves with its cool fern-like leaves, its seed pods gathered for a pretend meal in its shade. It was the meeting place when they made secret plans and always base when they played tag. She'd fallen from it when she was six and could still find the scar by her ankle if she searched hard enough. She'd sat under it for hours crying when *Mawmie* died and again when the last of

21

her siblings moved out.

This was her tree, alive and well again. Emily broke into tears, setting the box down on the table. Her shoulders shook with heavy sobs. Silas scooted his chair from the table with his knee out wide and grabbed Emily by the wrist. He pulled her to himself, allowing her to sit on his knee and cry on his shoulder as he petted her. She knew he was breaking the very rules he had set to comfort her, and she was grateful, allowing herself to be soothed by his strong arms.

Chapter 3

The snow was piling up quick. Silas paced back and forth, watching the driveway out the window of his house.

Where was she?

By the looks of the heavy clouds, school would be canceled for the rest of the day, and Emily should have been back by now. Once he'd made his mind up, it didn't take long to hitch up the buggy and ride down to the end of their long drive to find her.

There she was, her black *kapp* white with snow. Silas turned the buggy around as she turned up the drive.

She stopped to greet him. "I had to wait for all the students to be picked up."

Sometimes Silas wondered if the school would be the death of her.

"Well, get up to the house."

"Just let me get the mail," she said, "and then I'll be on."

"I'll get the mail, you get to the house." He knew he had no right to order her around like that. She wasn't his wife, and if anyone heard the way they talked to each other they'd probably be shunned for acting like it.

She smiled at him and flicked her wrists, sending the horse trotting up the drive.

Silas pulled the letters from both their mailboxes, tucking them in his coat. He put away the horses and a little later, met Emily in her warm kitchen to wait for supper.

Emily had changed into dry clothes, her *kapp* showing a thin band of her dark-red hairline above her forehead. A glimpse of her part, forever reminding him of her innocence.

"Did I get any mail?" she asked, moving pots and pans around.

"I almost forgot." Silas pulled the mail from his coat and separated it into two piles.

A curious letter stopped him. "Who's Clement Wickey?"

"I don't know," she said.

He held the letter in his hands, addressed to Emily Graber.

"Did you meet him today?" She set a heavy pan on the stove with a clank and turned back to the sink.

"No, but you got a letter from him."

Emily stopped what she was doing and came over, her eyes running all over the envelope now in her hands. She swallowed, a tell-tale sign she had an idea what it was about, then shoved the letter into her dress pocket.

Silas clenched his jaw. "Well, aren't you going to read it?"

"Later. I'm busy making supper right now." She stepped up to the sink, turning her back to him.

Silas felt his chest tighten. "Aren't you the least bit curious why a man would write you a letter?"

"*Nay*, it's probably just a cousin of mine I've forgotten about." Her voice was even-toned but edged with apprehension.

Silas stood and approached the sink. "Give it to me."

She turned around, eyebrows lowered and mouth dropped open, "I will do no such thing, Silas Moreland. It's my mail and I'll do what I want with it."

"We don't keep secrets, Emily. Open it."

After a tense stare, she withdrew the letter from her pocket. Walking away from him with a toss of her head, she sat down at the table and leaned back in the chair with the letter in front of her. "It says he'll be in the area next week and wants to know if I'd like to see a demonstration of a new type of washing machine invented by an Amish man in Gawson's Branch." She wadded the letter into a ball and stood. "Well, I simply don't have time for traveling salesmen."

As she made her way back to the sink he grabbed her around the waist and caught the wad of paper before it made its way back into her pocket.

Emily squealed. "Silas, let me go!"

With the letter now in his possession, he let her go. He smoothed it out on his pant-leg. "He's a widower with eight children, the youngest, a little girl who is four. It says here he wants permission to call on you. What does that mean, *call on?* We don't even have phones."

She snatched the letter from his hand. "It doesn't matter. I'm too busy for such nonsense."

"Do you get these letters often?" He stared at her wide-eyed.

"From time to time," she said quietly, fingering

the edge of her *kapp* behind her ear.

He should have known. How many chances had she had and thrown away? She was a beautiful woman with no excess baggage. He imagined every Amish widower in the state had looked for her address. But here she sat—miserable—all because of him.

"I think you should answer this one." The words came tumbling out before he'd even thought them through.

"*Nay*, Silas. I couldn't. I have my job."

He raised his voice slightly. "You've been moping around here for months and I know why. You miss having Natasha around. You could still have kids of your own, you know. It's not too late."

She eyed the letter in her hands.

"Who knows? This could be your last chance."

The look she gave him would haunt his dreams. It said, I know you're right, Silas. It was the first time in years he wished he were wrong.

Emily stared at Silas, the letter still in her hand. How had she not noticed the strands of white beginning in his beard before now? His hair was just beginning to gray at the temples. She still longed to run her hands through it as she had once, in this very kitchen, years ago, but old age was coming, and Silas was right. This could be her last chance.

She shook her head. It was complicated. She couldn't just leave Silas, even if he was telling her to.

"I love you," Emily said. Didn't that count for anything? They didn't say it often. In fact, it was a rare thing for them to discuss their relationship at all. Other than an occasional flirty comment and Silas mentioning that Emily would marry "one day", nothing was said about the pain that continued to fester between them. She had thought when Natasha came to stay that everyone was content and that they could survive the lifetime to follow. But now that she was gone, everything was different, leaving Emily unsure.

Silas wrapped his arms around her, holding her close. It was rare he touched her, much less held her, and for that reason alone the unsettled feeling began rising to the surface. She curled her arms in and allowed his warmth to spread all around her.

"I love you, too, Emily. I didn't want to see Natasha and Will go. It kills me to be away from my family. But I did what I thought was best for them. And this is what's best for you."

Did he think she was a child like Natasha and Will? Silent tears fell, dotting Silas's shirt. How many children had she taken care of over the years? And not one was her own. She didn't want to admit it, but Silas was right. She wanted a child of her own, and it was tearing her apart. But how could she leave him? She'd promised she wouldn't. "I won't leave you, Silas. Not ever."

"Yes, you will," he said sternly, holding her back now, just enough to see her face. He'd been using the same tone of voice that *vater* always used to correct his unruly *chinda*. "I've always told you the day would come. I can't handle it anymore, Emily. This is no kind of life for either one of us."

She winced at his words, knowing they were true. She knew it, but all this time she'd refused to believe it. Suddenly, her chest felt like lead and she struggled to breathe beneath the weight of Silas's arms.

She stared into his eyes. It was his fault. If he would have left the community, if he would have gone with Jada, he'd be nothing more than a faint memory to her by now. He'd ruined her life and her chances of ever being happy with anyone. She'd wasted her youth in a fantasy of a life she'd never have.

Gasping for air, Emily shook herself free of his embrace, cries of pain starting slowly, then morphing into an unidentifiable ringing in her ears, shaking her to her very core. Where were these feelings five years ago, or seven? Or any time before now when she could have done something about them?

Silas stood still, his eyes full of emotion, yet he made no further attempt to console her. She doubled over, feeling the pressure of her cries in her temple, and grabbed her *kapp* with both hands to somehow steady herself.

Her prayer kapp. The key to getting God to hear her prayers, but had He? Had He listened once over all these years when she went to Him for help with her hurting?

Heat flashed over her. She pulled the *kapp* off, ripping the pins out with it, and threw it to the floor, small strands of tangled hair hitting her in the face, further angering her. In a rage, she picked out all the other pins with trembling fingers and threw them across the room. They bounced with tiny clicks off the wall and down to the floor, her hair falling down heavy on her shoulders.

Her chest heaving, a helpless feeling of despair settled in her chest. It was wrong to be angry with God. The Lord would punish her for it, but what more could He possibly take from her?

She fell to her knees in a heap, searching her heart for a verse to bring her comfort. '*And God shall wipe away all tears from their eyes; and there shall be no more death, neither sorrow, nor crying, neither shall there be any more pain: for the former things are passed away.*'

She covered her face with her hands. Would she need to wait for death for comfort?

Silas rested a soft hand on her back, making her cries heavy again. She spied her head cover on the floor, and with regret at her actions, she motioned her fingers for Silas to retrieve it. He quickly handed it to her and she hugged it to her chest, trying hard not to pray. It was wrong to pray without it. She hoped God would forgive her for her anger. She'd done so much wrong already. It wasn't Silas's fault, or God's. It was hers. All hers. For lying. For kissing another woman's husband. For giving her heart to a forbidden man. And this was her punishment. To be sent away to marry someone she'd never love while always thinking of someone she'd never forget.

Rocking back and forth, comforting herself the only way she knew how, her cries quieted. Silas sat beside her silently on the floor, and she settled her eyes on the rip in the knee of his trousers she'd mended the week before. In a hurry, she'd not sewn the stitches straight. Now she wished more than anything she could go back and re-do them. How long would it be before Silas would rip another hole in his clothes, and who would be here to mend them?

Silas knocked on the door, but let himself in when Emily didn't appear. It'd been over a week since the big snow and the letter that changed everything. Neither of them had been the same since.

"Emily?" he called softly, not wanting to scare her. He peeked his head around the corner of the kitchen toward her bedroom. The door stood open; Emily lay on the bed, still sleeping. It was after ten. He stepped silently to the doorframe, her hair a flood of deep-red on the white sheet. Silas would give anything to have her for his wife—anything but his soul. Ironically, that was the one thing that would buy her.

But it wasn't just his soul at stake.

A flinch from Emily had him holding his breath. She turned her head to the side and curled into a ball. Beside her, the bed was empty, room enough for one more person. That familiar ache was back in his chest again. It was the same ache he had each night when he crawled into his own bed. How many nights he'd spent alone, but it was his fault. Mistakes Emily had never made, yet she had shared his fate the same. Well, no more.

Silas backed out of the hall slowly and let himself out the door. Closing it tightly, he returned to the yard, busying himself with things around the house he knew needed to be done, but didn't really care about anymore. Then, an hour later, he knocked on her door again.

A puffy-eyed Emily greeted him. Inside, he took off his hat and coat, and sat down at his usual seat at the table. "How are you?" he asked.

"Fine, and yourself?" She crossed her arms, holding onto one shoulder.

He looked down at the floor with a sigh. "Have you sent it yet?"

She sat down at the kitchen table, propping her head up with her hand. "I don't know what to say."

He nodded. "Maybe I could help you."

She stood, and with heavy-footed steps disappeared into the bedroom. A moment later she returned, plopping a notebook and pen on the table and loudly scooting her chair in.

"Dear Mr. Wickey," she said as she wrote. "Now what do you suggest?" Her eyes were hollow, staring right through Silas's.

"Just tell him you were happy to get his letter and mention your best qualities."

She blinked rapidly. "I have no best qualities right now."

"Tell him you're smart, and hardworking, brave, and the best cook ever."

Her eyes darted around. "Are you hungry? I was so busy I skipped breakfast this morning."

Silas placed his hand on her arm, but removed it

when she stared down at it intently. "I'm fine. I ate already."

"What did you eat?" she asked with narrowing eyes.

"A sandwich." It wasn't a total lie. He'd crumbled up some potato chips and wrapped it with a piece of bread. "What time did you get up this morning?" he asked.

"Oh, I don't know. Six or after."

A boldfaced lie. "Have you eaten?"

"I'm not hungry." She frowned at the notebook in front of her and began scribbling out more words. "I was happy to receive your letter and would enjoy meeting with you."

"Tell him you're a beautiful red-head."

"That would be incredibly vain. Besides, he may not want me at all if he knew I was red-headed."

"Why would you say that?" Silas squirmed in his chair. This was the last thing he wanted to be doing today, but if he didn't see to it that this letter got written, it might not.

"Most men don't like red hair."

He studied her. Was she serious? "You're the most beautiful woman I've ever met. If he doesn't like red-heads, don't even waste your time. Tell him." He nodded toward the paper.

She frowned and glanced down to the page once more. "I have red hair," she said as she wrote, "and?"

Silas waited for Emily to look up at him. "And eyes the color of tropical ocean water. Curves that lodge in a man's mind and keep him from a hard day's work. Lips that keep him from hearing what's been said. A gentle spirit. A faithful heart for God. And a longing for a life better than the one I can give her. It's what's right, Emily. And you're not wrong for wanting it."

"Then, why does it feel so wrong?" Her eyes were red now, and her voice strained.

He wished he knew.

"Silas, I don't know if I can do this." She was beginning to break down again. He couldn't let that happen.

He took hold of her hand on the table, setting the pen to the side. "'I can do all things through Christ which strengtheneth me.'"

Silas never thought he'd be encouraging Emily at her table with a Bible verse from memory. But so many things were happening now he never thought possible. He said a prayer that God would give them both strength for what was about to happen.

Clement Wickey showed Emily all around his home. It was big and open with lots of windows and more bedrooms than even Emily's house had. His wife, Ruby, had loved flowers and had many flower gardens all around the place, though nothing was growing yet.

It was peculiar that the man had decided to take Emily to meet his children on the first outing together. She wondered if she should see it as presumptuous or just practical. After all, it was important to get along

33

with the entire family, but having his children, aged four all the way up to sixteen, following them around everywhere left little time to socialize.

"Dawdie," little Melody said, her brown eyes big and beautiful. "Is Miss Emily going to stay for supper?"

Emily wanted to scoop the girl up in her arms and love her. She was a darling *chind* and so polite. It hurt Emily that she had lost her *mueter* at such a tender age. Her heart skipped a beat when she realized one day Melody might call her *mawmie*.

"I don't think so, Melody. Miss Emily and I have a lot to discuss. We'll be having supper in town tonight."

"May I have supper in town, too?"

Emily threw her hand up to her chest when the girl said may I. Most children these days say can I. Emily could already tell that Ruby was an attentive mother. How would Emily compare?

Clement laughed. "Not this time, dear."

Clement was a medium-sized man, stockily built with square shoulders. He was forty-five, a mite older than Emily, but he seemed lively and had a distinguished look about him that Emily thought she could get used to. He still had all his hair, though it was well streaked on the sides with gray, and his beard, though long, hadn't grown to crazy lengths like some men's beards did. Silas's was always very uniform for a man who never trimmed. Emily chastised herself for thinking of Silas at a time like this, blinking her eyes rapidly to remove the thought.

"Emily and I are going out for a while. I may be

back late. Emily's house is a long way from here and it'll take me a long time to get back."

His children all nodded silently and then wished their *dawdie* a good time as they went their separate ways through the house. Emily liked the order about the family, but something was a little off, and she couldn't put her finger on it. She studied on it all through supper at the same restaurant Nelson had taken her to, though she dared not tell Clement.

"Your children are delightful," Emily said.

"I can tell they really liked you, too."

"Where do they go to school?"

"They're homeschooled. Ruby wanted it that way. And it's one of the things I want to continue to do. The older girls take care of it now."

That was it. It seemed like the family was functioning well without the lady of the house, making Emily wonder if the man was simply lonely, looking for a companion. She took a bite of fried chicken, realizing then she'd only ordered it because it was Silas's favorite. What would be her role in a house that already functioned well? Silas and his children were so needy, and Emily hated to admit it, but she liked that. It made her feel wanted, and she loved to do things for them.

It was after dark when Clement returned Emily to her home. She knew he had a long way to go and it was cold outside. "I had a lovely time, Clement."

"Call me Clem." He didn't make arrangements to see her again, and she almost wished he wouldn't. Emily didn't want to fall in love again. She was still hurting from the first time.

In her room, Emily quickly changed into her nightgown and then carried the lantern into the kitchen. Silas was suddenly in front of the table, startling her.

"Sorry," he said, sitting down. "I just came to see how it went with Clement."

Normally, she'd be flattered by his jealousy, but this was serious. He was giving her over to another man and she didn't quite know what to think of it. "He wants me to call him Clem," she said, sitting down.

"What kind of name is Clement, anyway?" Silas wrinkled his nose.

She narrowed her eyes at him. "I don't know, *Ax,* perhaps he had no say in the matter."

He frowned, showing she had made her point. "Well, was he nice to you?"

"*Ja*, very nice."

"Well, everyone's nice on the first date," he mused.

"If it bothers you, I'll tell him to forget the whole thing." Emily wished for just that. The way Silas sat there made Emily want to throw her arms around him. She was almost tempted to cry, only to see if he would let her.

"No. Don't you dare. I'll behave. But you tell me if he tries anything with you. He didn't try to kiss you, did he?"

She raised her chin. "I don't believe in kissing until engagement."

"Well, I recall you kissing me." He grinned, and she looked away in embarrassment. "You've never kissed anyone else, have you?" His question was pointed.

She put her head down, her hands holding her forehead as she stared at the kitchen table.

"I stole that kiss from Clement, didn't I? I'm so sorry, Emily." His voice held true regret.

She raised her head boldly, grabbing a strand of her long hair at the very end with both hands. "I'm not," she said defiantly. She never would be, either. As wrong as it was, she would hold the memory forever in a place deep in her heart—a place Clement would never be allowed to go.

Spring arrived all too quickly, and Silas knew it wouldn't be long before the talk of wedding dates would come up. Emily and Clement weren't engaged yet, but he knew it could be any day. How would he live without his Emily? The thought made his breathing erratic, almost putting him into a panic attack. He didn't want to lose her, but keeping her wasn't an option. She needed to be free to live her own life. It was what her father would have wanted.

He watched Clement walk boldly into Emily's house. She was making him supper tonight. Emily had asked Silas if it was okay, saying if it bothered him she'd find a way out of it. He only wanted her to be happy, but why was her happiness causing him so much pain?

Silas got out the Bible, hoping there would be

something in there that could improve his mood. He wished it was his weekend to get the kids, though lately they had been too busy to come see him, even when it was his turn. How long before he was totally alone in the world again? He thought back to the Christmas he had very nearly taken his own life, wishing he could wake up tomorrow and have all his problems dissolved by the mighty hand of God.

Let me know I'm going to be okay, Lord.

He cried, knowing Clement sat on the very chair he wished was his at Emily's table.

Soon, he heard a knock at his door. He wiped his eyes on his shirt and answered it.

"Sorry to bother you, Silas," Emily said. "But the hitch has come loose on Clem's buggy and he's got a long way to go. Could he borrow some tools?"

"No problem," Silas said, trying to appear normal. He shook the man's hand.

"I've heard a lot about you," Clement said.

Silas certainly hoped not. "Oh?" He glanced at Emily.

"*Ja,* Emily says you do most of the work around here and she helps out with your children sometimes."

"Right. She's a good neighbor. Let me get my coat and I'll get you those tools."

Outside, they all started for the tool shed when Clement suggested Emily wait in the house. Silas caught a hesitant gaze from her as she walked away.

"Use whatever you need," Silas said, the tool shed open now. Clement grabbed a tool and they walked together to the buggy.

"Emily is a real nice lady," Clement said,

stopping when he reached the hitch.

"Yeah, she is." *And if you ever hurt her I'll hunt you down...*

"I can tell she's very fond of your family."

Silas hoped Emily hadn't tried to lie to Clement. The horrible liar she was, no telling what Clement thought. *Cover a lie with honesty.* "My daughter is dyslexic and was three years behind in her schoolwork, but when Emily started working with her she caught right up. She taught her to cook, too."

"Are you a widower as well?"

Apparently, Emily hadn't told Clement as much as he thought. "No, she left the community." It was embarrassing to say, and Silas tried to steer conversations away from it when he could.

"I'm sorry to hear that. It hurts to lose your wife."

Silas felt an instant bond with the man. Not only had they been through similar experiences, Clement didn't put him down for his wife leaving him. As much as he wanted to hate the guy, he couldn't, making the situation even more confusing. "I'm glad Emily's found a good man to spend time with. She deserves that."

Clement's eyes scanned Silas up and down and then handed the tool back to him. "*Ja*, she does. It was *guete* to meet you, Silas." He shook his hand again and then went back to Emily's house.

Emily waited anxiously for Clement to come back inside and tell her goodbye. She knew he would since he left the container of cookies she made for the children on the counter. He'd spent several minutes talking with Silas alone and the suspense of not knowing what was being said made her sick at her stomach.

Finally, Clement came through the door, knocking once before entering. "Did you get it fixed?" she asked.

"*Ja*. Only a small matter, nothing for you to worry about."

Realizing she must look anxious for him to say that, she relaxed the muscles in her face. "Well, you just have such a long way to go."

He stood close to her. "*Ja*, it's a shame our houses have to be so far from each other." His eyes were drifting around her face.

Her pulse sped. She wanted to kiss him. Could it be she was falling for the man so quickly? It had only been a few months they'd been courting. She glanced at his lips, inviting her near. They'd both agreed it was only proper not to touch until engagement, but they were so tempting. Could his kisses help her forget about Silas? If so, she wanted them now.

Clem smiled knowingly. "I think I'd better go now, Emily. The children will be waiting." He nodded before exiting the kitchen door.

Emily took a deep breath and exhaled slowly. So many things clouded her mind. This was what was supposed to happen, yet she felt guilty for having feelings for another man. She went into the bedroom and quickly changed for bed. When she returned to the kitchen, Silas was sitting at the table.

"You shouldn't be seeing me in my nightgown," she said to him casually, though it had happened often enough it didn't even startle her anymore.

"I like to see you in your nightgown," he said playfully, but his eyes were sad.

"What's wrong?"

"It's Clement."

"Don't you like him?"

He nodded. "That's the problem. I don't know if it would be easier if he were a jerk or a prince."

A knock at the door stopped their conversation cold. Their eyes met only a split second before Silas jumped up and ran out of the kitchen toward the back hall, leaving Emily in control of answering the door in her nightgown. She swallowed her heart, which had lodged itself uncomfortably in her throat. Getting close to the door she called out in a shaky voice, "Who is it?"

"It's me, Clement. I'm sorry, Emily, I forgot the cookies you made on the counter."

Emily grabbed the cookies and rushed back to the door. "I'm-uh, in my nightgown, Clem." Her voice was pitchy and her breathing erratic.

"Oh, I'm sorry, Emily. It's okay."

"Wait," she said. "I'll hand them to you out the door." She opened the door a crack and pushed them out, her dark hair flowing down her arm in the moonlight. He took the container from her, brushing her hand as he did, sending a shiver up her spine. "Are you okay?" he said quietly, his face close to the crack.

"*Ja*, you just...startled me, that's all." Emily swallowed hard.

"I thought I heard you talking to someone."

Her spine stiffened. She could see only the corner of his mouth and his long beard from where she stood. What could she say? "I talk to myself a lot. It's kind of embarrassing, but it gets a little creepy after dark in this big house and talking helps me." She laughed nervously. "Sometimes I even sing."

"Ah, I see. Well, I'm sorry to have frightened you."

"It's okay, Clem."

"*Goot nacht.*"

"Good night." Emily shut the door and locked it, then hurried straight to the living room door and locked it as well. She hadn't locked the doors in years, but maybe she should start.

She took the lantern into her bedroom and shut the door, locking it, too. "Silas, you can come out now," she whispered, her nerves still making her jittery. She figured he'd be hiding in the shadows somewhere, this being the closest room to the kitchen and knowing full well Clement should never be visiting it.

"Are you sure?" His low voice escaped the closet.

"Of course I'm sure."

He emerged, almost tripping on the way out. "Did you see him leave?"

"Well, not exactly."

"Then put out that lamp!" he demanded.

"You're being ridiculous," she said, but blew

out the lamp just in case. She sat down on the bed, feeling Silas's back almost to hers. She laid down.

"I *really* shouldn't be *here*. What did he say?" Silas's voice was low and secretive.

"He heard voices and I told him it was me talking to myself."

"I'll bet you five bucks he's waiting outside for someone to come out of the house."

She slapped at his arm. "He is not."

He turned toward her. "If you were my woman, I'd wait all night."

Emily began to worry that Silas may be right. She had no idea of the inner workings of a man's brain, after all. "Then stay here and we'll talk awhile before you go. His children will be waiting on him, he can't stay out there forever."

Silas lay down beside her. "They could stone us for this. Or they'd tar and feather me and burn you at the stake like a witch." Silas's panicked whisper set her oddly at ease.

She turned to the side and placed her hand on his chest, feeling his heart pound. "I think you were more scared than I was." She giggled.

"This isn't funny, Emily. I almost got us caught. All because I couldn't wait till tomorrow to know your business."

"Is that why you come? I thought it was because you missed me." Emily didn't know why she was so comfortable with Silas in her bed. It would be a terrible thing if anyone found out, but it seemed Silas was worried enough for the both of them.

"Has he tried to kiss you yet?" It was something Silas asked after each outing, and the answer was always *nay*.

"He did," Silas said when she hesitated.

"*Nay*, he didn't. But I wanted to kiss him." Her tone was serious, putting tension back in the room. Silas had been honest about Jada, and now it was her turn. And maybe if he were jealous he'd rethink this whole thing and tell her not to do it.

She could hear him swallow in the dark. "Do you think he'll make a good husband to you?"

"I do." She didn't want to admit it, but there was nothing wrong with Clem or his family, and she was beginning to have feelings for him. His children were caring and pleasant people, and little Melody needed a *mueter*. It hurt her heart just thinking about it. If only things were different. If only she had two lives to live, she'd spend at least one with Silas.

"Do you ever wonder why there's no marriage in Heaven?" Emily asked.

"Because there's no arguing allowed?" Silas turned to face her, wiggling himself comfortable on the big bed.

"We don't argue."

"Sometimes we do, but I like to see you all riled up."

Her eyes had adjusted to the darkness now, and she could see him faintly watching her with serious eyes. He ran his fingers through the hair above her ear.

"How wrong would it be if I kissed you once more?" she asked, her eyes getting misty from thoughts of saying goodbye to him forever.

"I was wondering the same thing. We'd better not, though. I'm sure it would only lead to more regrets." He continued to brush her hair with his fingers, and she began to cry. She'd shed so many tears in the last few months, she wondered how there could possibly be any more. Scooting closer to him, she rested her head on his chest, draping her arm around him, and with silent tears, surrendered to sleep.

Chapter 4

Emily couldn't wait for summer, but somehow when May came, she found she still couldn't shake the winter blues. Her feelings for Clem had grown and now she was in love with two men, but only one could give her the family she longed for.

Please, God. Give me the heart I need to do your will.

Leaving Silas would be the hardest thing she ever had to do, and to be honest with herself, she wasn't sure she could go through with it.

"Has he asked you yet?" Silas said carefully.

"Nay." He'd stopped coming into her house after each outing, leaving him to wonder until they met on the porch the next day for meals. In fact, Silas hadn't been in her house except to fill the wood rack since the time they were almost caught together by Clem and ended up sleeping together in Emily's bed. Well, Emily slept. Silas was gone in the morning, and she still didn't know how long he'd stayed.

Silas smashed a tick between his thumbnails and wiped it on his pants. "How long does courting usually last?"

She shook her head at him in disgust. "It varies. There's no set rule about it. Are you trying to get rid of me?"

"Yes," he said matter-of-factly.

"Thanks."

"I've been praying a lot about it and I just had to give it up to God. We both want what's best for you and I think He can do a better job than I can."

So he was content? The thought was both

welcomed and troubling at the same time.

"Well, you better get home before he gets here. I've left your supper on the stove."

"Going to Wheezie's again?"

"I have no idea."

"Well, have a good time."

Watching Silas go was surreal. Her heart often threatened to quit beating in protest whenever she thought about him. Then, in an instant, she could forget all about Silas and have a good time with Clem. It was almost as if she had two destinies planned for herself, and she hadn't yet told her mind she had to choose. And Emily knew the time was drawing near.

Clem had been acting odd most of the evening. Emily had carried on most of the conversation at the restaurant, and now on the buggy ride home, he hadn't said anything for miles. Finally, Emily had to ask, "Have I done something wrong?"

"*Nay*, why do you ask?"

"You're just usually so much more talkative."

Clem stopped the buggy and swatted at a mosquito. He turned to her. "I'm sorry, Emily. I've had a lot on my mind today." He drew closer to her, the sun setting over the horizon, making the whole sky appear to have an orange glow to it. She gazed into his eyes and felt the pull that had her wanting to kiss him. She wondered what Clem would think of her if she just went for it, but Amish men weren't used to women dominating them. And how would she explain herself if he didn't approve?

"Emily, I want you to join our family, and be my wife."

This was it. The moment her life would change forever. Was she ready to make the decision, and would she live to regret it? His eyes held her captive. She wanted to kiss him so badly, if for no other reason than to know how to answer. With sweaty palms, she leaned in and kissed him on the mouth. A surge of excitement ran through her at the parting of his lips. Letting herself go, she kissed him more, but then he stopped her. Their eyes locked as she breathed in a heavy breath, the whole experience leaving Emily confused, rather than empowered with a solid decision.

"I'll take that as a yes," he said, smiling. He took the reins up and they began down the road again.

What had she done? After thinking about it for months and deciding already she would say yes, she now felt the decision was careless and rushed. He said goodnight and left her on her porch alone with her thoughts.

Emily sat there for half an hour or more, swatting at mosquitoes before she went inside. She knew Silas wouldn't be visiting her at night anymore, so she decided to go see him.

"May I come in?" Emily said from Silas's door. He knew she'd just made it back from her date, not more than an hour ago. Holding the door open wide, he watched her hips sway as she crossed the kitchen to the living room where she plopped herself down in his favorite spot.

"Is something wrong?" He debated with himself if it would be a good or bad thing if she and Clement had a nasty break-up.

"He proposed." She watched him with eyes like an owl. "I thought you'd want to know."

He sat down next to her. This was the moment he'd waited for. God had been preparing his heart for this to happen and he hoped he was strong enough. "Did you give him an answer?"

Her eyes shifted about like they did when she told a lie, but there was no reason for her to lie about this. She was just unsure about her decision. *"Nay."*

He let out the breath he was holding. It was up to him to make this easier on both of them. But first—one last kiss before she forever belonged to another.

He drew near, knowing he'd need to use major restraint, his body already re-living the heat of kissing her before. His breathing became heavy in his chest as he took her small cheek in his calloused hand. He would kiss her gently on the lips and free her forever.

His thumb touched her bottom lip, sending his strength failing already. Harder than he intended, he kissed Emily on the mouth; his mind warned him to resist, but his body refused. She ran her fingers through his hair as she pressed deeper, almost sending him over the edge of no return. Emily was his no longer. It was time for him to say goodbye. He released her, his forehead to hers and with heavy breaths from them both, Emily intertwined the fingers of their hands.

It took Silas a moment to be able to speak. "I promise not to interfere with you and Clem. Don't tell me what happens between you two. You'll not cook or clean for me anymore."

Emily frowned as a tear fell, their hands still together, but he wasn't finished. "Don't come into my house, and we'll each keep our doors locked at night." He felt a tear slide down, making his voice a cracked whisper. *Help me, God, to be strong.* "I wish you all the joy and happiness in the world, and I will never, ever forget you, but I think it's best if we never speak of it again."

"Oh, Silas," she cried.

He let her hands go and stood, raising his voice. "Not another word, even when we're alone. No letters, no secret codes—nothing. I won't interfere with your marriage." Feeling the walls closing in on him, he knew he had to get out of the house. "Goodbye, Emily."

He darted outside and started walking, not sure where he was going. Finally, he wandered to the barn where the extra pieces of the mimosa stump still littered the corner. He picked one up and threw it across the barn, then punched the wall, sinking down to sitting position on the dirt floor. It reminded him of how Job dressed in sackcloth and sat in ashes in the Bible. With his head down, he took a handful of dirt and poured it over his hair. *This is me, God. At my lowest.* But he knew it wasn't. He'd been in worse places before. And though the temptation to go there again was strong, right now he'd settle for sackcloth and ashes. He poured the dirt on top his head with both hands, hoping God would see him, but knowing it wouldn't change a thing.

He waited there an hour or more, partly because he needed to be sure Emily wasn't still in his house, and because he really didn't know what to do with himself. He was all alone again. Silas thought back to the time he and Emily had fallen in the mud chasing cows before church and how pretty she looked. He knew he had done the right thing by giving her to Clem, but why did it feel so wrong?

He entered his house and on the place where Emily had last sat was an envelope. Gritting his teeth, he picked it up. He'd told her no letters. Why couldn't she just do as he told her? He opened it to find a lock of dark-red hair. Amish women never even trimmed their hair, and Emily had wanted him to have a piece of it. Did she really think he could ever forget her?

Silas was brought to tears, praying to God to take away his misery, and heal his broken heart, yet again. He thought in the barn that he might be okay, that he had a chance to heal, but did he?

Slamming the bedroom door, he paced back and forth, wondering what he should do next. How was he supposed to feel?

His eyes found the shelf. It was calling to him, just like it always did when things got bad. Remembering his pledge never to go there again didn't make the urge go away. But he wasn't that man anymore, was he? Maybe if he just held it in his hands he'd see how stupid it was. Impulsively, he walked over to the shelf and reached up, but he didn't feel it. He stood on his tiptoes and peered over the high shelf. The gun was gone.

"You seem distant," Clem said as he brought her home one hot afternoon after a picnic with all the children.

The wedding was fast approaching and Emily was still torn. How could she leave either of the men she loved? "I'm just really stressed about the wedding."

"Well, I guess that's to be expected, seeing it's your first."

She knew he hadn't meant anything by it, but the reminders that he had been married before made her uncomfortable. He was a good man, and it was nice that he hadn't forgotten his wife. She hoped he would forgive her for not ever forgetting her first love, either.

It had been two weeks since he'd proposed. Two long weeks since Silas had kissed her and told her to leave and not come back. Of course, it was for her own good, but it cut her deeply. She'd hoped when she came over he would tell her not to say yes to Clem, which was why she lied to him about not giving him an answer yet. She hadn't expected him to say goodbye this soon, though. There were so many things she couldn't say. She could never tell him she loved him anymore or that she'd always be here for him. She'd never again be able to tell him how nice he looked in his going-out clothes, or tease him about wanting to kiss him. And who could she talk things out with, if not Silas?

"I just want things to be right, you know?" She looked to Clem for comfort, hoping he'd understand she needed some reassurance.

"Do you want to set the wedding back?"

She knew it was a question, rather than a suggestion, but Emily had to take what she could get. "You'd do that for me? Clem, that's so sweet of you to understand."

He gave a thin smile. "Will a month more do?"

"*Ja*, that'd be perfect." Emily would be sure in another month, especially if she couldn't speak to Silas all that time.

At her door, she wondered if Clem would kiss her. She hoped he would, helping to keep him in her mind through the week, instead of Silas. He leaned in and kissed her gently, and Emily reached up to touch his hair when Clem stopped her, grabbing her wrist. "I can see we need to move that wedding date up instead of back," he whispered, rubbing her hand.

Emily's cheeks burned hot. "I'm sorry, I didn't mean to be so forward."

"I can understand. You've been alone in this house for far too long."

She could feel his eyes dancing around her body. She had been, hadn't she? It had caused her mind to go to unholy places. And while she'd never told a lie as a child, she found herself lying through her teeth ever since she met Silas. This was what was best for her, she just wished God would tell her heart, so it would know, too.

A month flew by, putting Emily back in the same situation she had been in. Two weeks until the wedding and she still didn't feel right about any of it. She'd prayed for peace but found none. The hot sun of August beat down on Emily's *kapp* where she worked in the garden with Natasha. It was rare that she visited anymore and Emily hadn't seen Will in months.

"How's your *mueter*?" Emily asked.

"She's doing pretty good. Getting along with my step-dad, anyway."

"Well, that's good to hear." Emily wondered about Jada's diet. "Does she ever just go off the deep end sometimes and eat bacon or anything?"

Natasha laughed. "Sometimes she goes crazy eating organic candy, but that's about it."

"Do you eat meat when you're at home?" She wondered how much the girl had changed since she'd gone back to living an *Englisher* life.

"I cook for myself, usually, and Will's never home."

Emily pressed her lips together. "I'm sorry to hear that." She wished for Natasha to have a happy family. Even now, if Natasha wanted to move into the community, Emily would rarely see her. It was like she was saying goodbye to her as well.

"Listen, has Dad said anything to you about not feeling well?"

Emily sat up straight. "*Nay*, I haven't talked to him much lately, though. He probably just has spring allergies." Emily knew the real reason. That when their

54

hearts both shattered they'd picked up the wrong pieces, and now there was no putting themselves back together again. Would either of them ever heal completely?

"I hope so. I know you're busy with getting things ready for the wedding and all, but if you wouldn't mind checking on him, it would make me feel better."

How could Emily tell Natasha she couldn't? That it was just too painful? "*Ja*. Of course." Emily watched the girl work, trying to say goodbye to her in her mind. She was so different now, so grown up. She wasn't Emily's child, but for a time she'd loved her like she was. And now it was time to love a new group of children the same way, and possibly have one of her own. This was exactly what she wanted, wasn't it?

Another picnic with Clem and his children at their home set Emily's mind at ease, some. The wedding was in a week, and as long as little Melody sat on her lap, Emily was calm and reassured, but when the girl jumped up to go play, leaving Emily alone with Clem, Emily's nerves acted up again.

They sat on an outstretched blanket in the yard, Clem's toes wiggling in the sunshine. *Dawdie* had gone barefoot in the yard, too, but she'd only seen Silas's bare feet in the house. There were many differences between the two men. Silas was taller, with deep-brown eyes, instead of blue. Clem kissed her respectfully; Silas kissed with a maddening passion that curled her toes. Clem had offered her a family; Silas wasn't even allowed to be inside her house without witnesses. The right thing to do was to give her heart to Clem.

"What's on your mind?" Clem asked.

"Nothing, why?" Emily took in her surroundings, trying to bring herself back to the conversation she was supposed to be having with her betrothed.

"You've been staring off into space for a while now."

"I have? I'm sorry. This wedding must have me frazzled."

"That's what you said a month ago. I hope you're not backing out on me." His smile indicated he was only teasing.

"Nay." She wished she could ask for another month, but knew it probably wouldn't make a difference. She gazed into his eyes but saw a wall. Clem was like a great open field to be explored, but only after she'd gotten past the gate. She knew everything about Silas: his past, his bad habits, his pain, and the joy of serving him. Now it was time to learn all those things about Clem.

One week before Emily's wedding to Clem, Silas sat doubled over in his living room with a headache like an ax to his skull. It made him sick to think of Emily being with another man. So sick he couldn't eat or work. It was all he could do to keep up with the chores around the house and he was out of practice when it came to cooking.

A knock at the kitchen door brought him to his feet quickly, making the pain in his head worse. He walked over and opened it. Emily stood looking at him. His stomach heaved.

"Silas, you don't look so good."

He turned around and trudged back to his place in the living room, plopping down with his head in his hands. "What do you need, Emily?" He'd been sharp with her for a while now, forcing a distance between them.

"Natasha said I should check in with you, that you weren't feeling well. I didn't realize you were actually sick."

"I'm fine."

Emily reached for him. "Let me feel."

He glanced up at her. "I said I'm fine."

She put her hand on his forehead anyway. "You're burning up. I think you should go to the doctor."

So he really was sick. He thought he was just missing Emily. "It's probably just a stomach bug. It'll go away in a day or two. You should go before I give it to you."

"I could make you some soup."

"No—no cooking. Don't you have things to do?" He hated to be harsh with her, but it was for her own good. She didn't need to be babying him when she had a wedding to get ready for. And he didn't want her pity.

"I'll check on you again tomorrow." Emily walked out of the room without so much as a goodbye. Silas made his way to the bedroom, collapsing his aching body on the bed, wishing Emily could pet him and feed him soup. As if his life wasn't bad enough the way it was, now he had the stomach flu.

"Go to the doctor, Silas." Emily stood over Silas's bed, watching him in nothing but his trousers. He'd been really sick for at least three days now, and it seemed to be getting worse.

"I can't. I've got chores to do." Silas's face was pale and he was so weak. He wasn't even making an effort to get out of the bed. She wondered how he'd ever make it through his chores at this rate. "I'll get someone to do your chores if you'll go see the doctor."

He sat up slowly with his face staring at the ceiling. For a while, he didn't move at all. "Okay," he said finally.

That one word ignited fear in Emily. If Silas was going to the doctor instead of doing his chores, he really was in bad shape.

"Can I get someone to take you?" Emily certainly couldn't do it, not without being the talk of the settlement.

"No."

"Are you sure you can make it there by yourself?" She wished Will or Natasha was here to go with him.

"Yeah. I'm fine." He grabbed his shirt from the

side table and held it up. And when he struggled with it, Emily helped to pull it around and held it out for him to slide his arm in the other sleeve.

"You shouldn't be in here," he said.

She ignored him completely, helping him fasten the snaps. "I'll go get the buggy ready."

In a few minutes, she was sending him out by himself, praying he had the presence of mind to make it to town and back safely.

She fed and watered the chickens and carried in wood for the cookstoves in each house. Silas's place was a mess, but she knew he'd have a fit if she cleaned it.

Soon, Clem arrived and Emily had a choice. She could ride out and ask someone to take care of Silas's chores, or ask Clem to help her do it. Clem listened intently as she explained. He agreed, and they started for the horses first. "I've never done chores like this with a pretty lady before." Clem pumped water for the trough as he watched her.

"Well, I usually prefer to work indoors, myself, other than the garden."

"What do we do next?" he asked.

"Feed the pigs."

"Your neighbor has quite a little farm here."

"It's all organic, too." She walked with Clem over to where the young piglets were.

"Do you help with Silas's chores often?" Clem had a curious look in his eye.

"Nay," she said self-consciously. "But I did

help make sure everything got done when Silas had to leave for several weeks, once."

"How is it that you two came to live…so close?"

Was he onto her? "This whole property used to be owned by the Hiltys. My house was the main house and Silas's was built on later as a *dawdiehouse*, for the Hiltys' aging parents. When they sold the property, they split it, deciding no one else would ever want two houses, and my *vater* bought one of them. Later on, Silas and his wife purchased the other."

"How long ago was that?"

"I was fifteen."

"So he's lived here a long while, then."

"*Ja*, he and *Dawdie* were very close, and when *Dawdie* died, Silas took on a lot of the outdoor chores for our place." Emily hoped Clem would understand she was indebted to Silas a great deal.

"Well, I have grown sons who help me with chores when I'm ill. I couldn't imagine not having anyone." Clem's words stabbed Emily's heart. Who would help Silas when she left?

"*Ja*, it's sad, really. He's a good man. I wish his son would visit more."

"Well, I think we should finish these chores so we can visit some more."

Emily smiled. "You're right." It was time to set thoughts of Silas aside. She was marrying Clem in four days, and all this would soon be her former life.

Three days later Emily sat on the edge of Silas's

bed, counting the pills in the little bottle.

"I told you, I'm taking them like they said." Silas looked like death. His eyes were hollow, his face a sickly pale color, and he hardly moved.

"Then why are you getting worse instead of better?" She walked into the kitchen with a rag and ran it under the cool water, wringing it out thoroughly before returning.

"I don't know," he said wearily.

She folded the rag and laid it on his forehead. "You should go back to the doctor."

"I've already been to the doctor and they couldn't help me."

"Well, what exactly did they say was wrong with you?" She'd never seen anyone this sick before. The man could barely stand he was so weak, and his fever still hadn't broken yet.

"They don't know for sure, but they thought it had to do with the bite." His words stopped her.

"What bite?"

"The one on my leg."

Emily held her arms over her stomach. "Show me."

"I'm not showing you. It's a tick bite on the inside of my leg and it's red and swollen. They said these pills would help," he mumbled.

She eyed him again. He had barely left his bedroom since he returned from the doctor. She'd finally gotten him to agree to let her feed him some homemade vegetable soup. "Silas, this is serious."

"If it's my time to go, what say do I have?" His eyes were closed as he talked. He complained of constant nausea, made worse by any movement. Someone would be arriving soon to do Silas's chores for the morning. If it was Leo, he'd sit with him awhile. She couldn't let anyone find her in Silas's bedroom. "I'll check on you again later."

Silas didn't respond.

With heavy steps, Emily went out to the porch swing and sat down, picturing Silas where he always sat on the top step. Tomorrow she'd be married and this wouldn't even be her home anymore. She'd packed a bag of her clothes and a few personal belongings, including the wooden box Silas had made for her. Soon, she and Clem would go through everything in the house together and see what they wanted to keep. Emily wondered how Silas was doing, itching to go check on him again.

God, remember Silas. He needs You and he still has a family that needs him.

A buggy pulled into the drive, and Clem jumped down, smiling as he headed toward her. "What are you up to, little lady?" he said as he sat down next to her on the swing, grabbing her hand. She glanced at him and then to their hands. He wasn't usually so affectionate.

"What? I can't hold my wife's hand?" he asked.

"It won't be official until tomorrow," she said with a shaky stomach. Perhaps she would get what Silas had, buying her another week or so.

"What's wrong? You're not your usual perky self."

"Silas is very sick."

"Still yet?"

"*Ja*, they gave him antibiotics, but he's only getting worse. I'm afraid for him." She was fighting back tears just talking about it.

Clem turned to Emily, directing her chin with the side of his finger. "If it's the Lord's will, he'll get better soon. It's not for you to worry about."

She tried getting lost in his eyes, wishing she could believe his words. He kissed her gently and then Emily put her arm around him, laying her head on his shoulder. Heart pounding, she knew better than to ask, but she opened her mouth anyway. "Please, Clem. Can we put the wedding off, just until Silas is better? He has no one and I'm afraid for him." It was true. What if Silas died alone in that bed, all because she didn't have the heart to ask Clem to move back the wedding?

"Emily, are you sure you want to marry me?" His voice held no sympathy.

She sat up straight. "*Ja*, I am. I just…it doesn't feel right to leave him like this."

"You're a good woman, Emily Graber, but you need someone to take care of you. Silas can take care of himself."

She nodded, not daring to go against him. It wasn't their way. He would be her husband in less than a day, and she'd be bound to obey his will until death parted them.

After Leo Schwartz had done Silas's chores for the evening and darkness descended on both their houses, Emily tiptoed into Silas's bedroom. She didn't want to wake him if he was sleeping, but she had to know how he was doing. She found him asleep on his stomach on the bed, his shirt off, with only his trousers on. His bare feet hung off the side of the bed. He didn't look good at all. Emily wondered if he were awake or asleep.

He moaned in pain. Rushing to his bedside, she knelt down, pushing his hair out of his eyes. He opened them slightly, then closed them again. "Emily?" he said weakly. "I don't feel well."

"Oh, Silas. What can I do for you?"

"Nothing. What day is it?"

"Sunday."

"A church Sunday?" he asked.

"*Nay*. A visiting Sunday."

Silas didn't even know what day it was, how could he fend for himself?

"Silas, I can get an ambulance to come and take you to the hospital."

"No. The Lord will take me or he won't."

Emily huffed at the stubborn man in front of her. She went into the kitchen and brought back a chair from the table, setting it right by his bed. Then, she wet the cloth with cool water and sat down beside him, preparing herself for a long night.

Chapter 5

Silas tried to silence the alarm clock that was driving nails into his skull, but couldn't seem to reach it. His eyes opened and Emily was rolling her head around in a chair beside his bed. She glanced at him absentmindedly and then grabbed the alarm clock, nearly beating it to get it to shut off. "Sorry to wake you, Silas," she said.

What was she doing in his bedroom? "What is today?"

She glanced to the floor and then back at him. "Monday."

He jerked his head up to see the clock, surprised at the strength it took from him. Six a.m. Her wedding to Clement started at eight. He rolled to his side, his stomach remaining horizontal.

"How are you feeling?"

What did it matter how he was feeling? Her wedding was about to start. "You need to go now, Emily." All his strength went into speaking; he hoped she didn't make him say it twice.

"I don't want to leave you like this, Silas."

"I'll be fine. Just go."

She felt of his forehead and then brought him a fresh rag, tears in her eyes. He knew this was hard for her, but it had to be. Clement and her new life were waiting for her and he wouldn't let his illness stand in the way of her happiness. She stared at him like she was going to burst if she didn't say something.

"Go, Emily. Now," he said as firmly as he could. He watched her leave his room, realizing that not only was she not coming back, but that if he succumbed to sleep again, he may never wake up.

Emily sat under the young mimosa tree wondering the whole time why there wasn't a right answer. It didn't seem to matter which way she went, she'd be unhappy. It was time to leave for her wedding and she wasn't sure if she should even go. Touching the tree one last time, she turned and walked inside. She grabbed her bag and sat down at the table with it in her arms. Her eyes darted around her kitchen. So many memories. *Mawmie* had taught her to cook right over there at the woodstove, and *Dawdie* drank coffee and read the newspaper on the chair beside her. She could still see his grin when he teased her about her red hair. The memories would still live on when she cooked in Clem's kitchen, but would they be as vivid?

Her head turned to the spice cabinet and to a moment of sin she'd never forget. It shouldn't be listed with the happy memories, but it was, making it sinful even to this day.

Emily stood and commanded her feet to take her to the buggy.

Down the road the buggy rumbled, faster and faster, before she could think any more on it and change her mind. It was times like these she wished she had someone else's opinion. She had Silas's. He was telling her to go get married, but the further she traveled from the house, the further she felt her heart was.

About halfway there she felt the unmistakable pull of Silas behind her and in her mind saw the paleness of his skin where she'd left him so helpless on the bed. Overcome with anguish, she stopped the buggy in the middle of the road and prayed. *God, please tell me what to do. I place my life in Your hands, and You hold Silas's life, too. Tell me what to do, and this time, I promise to obey.*

Silas closed his eyes again, *God, take my life from me. My wife left me years ago, my kids rarely visit, and now Emily's marrying another man. I have nothing to live for, so if it's Your will, receive me with open arms.*

And with that, Silas gave himself to God to do as He pleased. A calmness washed over him and he let himself go with it. Was this what death felt like, or was this the arms of Jesus?

"Silas?" an unfamiliar voice called to him. "Silas? Can you hear me?"

Silas opened his eyes, not concerned with the two strangers in his home.

"We're here to help you. Can you tell us your name?" The man felt his wrist and gave a tense glance to the woman beside him.

"Silas," he managed to mutter.

"What's your full name? Can you tell us that?"

Silas tried, but he couldn't remember. He shut his eyes again, remembering the peacefulness he'd felt when he gave his problems to God, hoping to return to that safe place.

"What's wrong with him?" Emily cried.

"We don't know. You said he had a tick bite?"

"*Ja*, on the inside of his leg."

"We're taking him in," he told the woman beside him. "Get the stretcher."

Emily's heart lurched at the thought of him leaving. There was no way she could let him go to the hospital all alone; she was coming, too. "Could I ride with you?" she asked.

"Yes," the man said. "Immediate family is allowed."

Emily ran to the kitchen. She was about the closest family Silas had right now, and no one was going to stop her. She scribbled out a note and taped it to the window, *Went with Silas to the hospital.* There was no time to even think about what else to say. She climbed into the back of the ambulance after Silas, hoping he'd forgive her for what she'd just done.

The woman drove the ambulance while the man attended to Silas. It was strange to be in the back of such an odd, enclosed space with a man. Silas was out cold, leaving Emily to trust the man would take care of him.

"Is he going to be okay?" she asked. She watched the man put a mask over Silas's face, making him look even frailer.

"He's going into shock."

Shock? Emily pictured a person with a seizure. "But he looks so calm."

"It means his blood pressure has dropped too low. He's not getting enough oxygen to sustain his body. It looks like we may have gotten here just in time."

"So you can help him?"

"I hope so." The man had rubber gloves on and was injecting a syringe of something into Silas's arm. She grabbed Silas's hand, knowing these people thought he was her husband anyway. She prayed, *God, please save Silas. He's my best friend.*

Every hallway in the hospital seemed the same, an unending maze of white doors and *Englishers* dressed in the same strange outfits, men and women alike. This wasn't a place she should be without someone else from the community, but she knew they'd be arriving soon enough, and the thought made her insides roll.

Around a corner, a stocky bald man nearly ran into her. "Excuse me," he muttered as he stepped around her, but his voice sounded a lot like Silas's creep-friend, Kenny Z. Emily straightened herself and found a desk. A serious woman with a painted smile said Emily would need to wait for Silas to get a room, but she offered to let her use the phone.

After the calls were made, Emily found the place they wanted her to sit. The faces in the room were all cold and unfriendly. It was half an hour before she was allowed to see Silas. The woman gave her a room number and sent her on a long journey down three halls and up a floor.

Inside, she found a helpless-looking Silas in a narrow, white bed, tubes hooked to him on both sides. She stood beside the bed, taking his cold, limp hand in hers. "Oh, Silas. Please don't die," she whispered. His eyes opened, but only partway. They were so glazed over from all the things they had given him already, and Emily wondered if he could even hear her. Then they found hers and she sensed his deep hurt. The oxygen mask wouldn't allow him to speak anyway, but she doubted he even had the strength. She needed to tell him what was on her heart before the others came. "Silas, I'd rather be your friend forever, than to marry anyone else. I promise never to leave you again. I mean it this time. This is my decision, and God has given me peace about it."

Silas squeezed Emily's hand gently, bringing joy to her heart.

The knock at the door caused Emily to jump to attention. She let go of Silas's hand immediately.

Jada entered, followed by Natasha and Will. "How is he?" Jada asked, eyeing her sharply.

"He's very weak." Emily thought of the soft way he'd squeezed her hand.

Jada examined him closer, combing his hair back with her fingers. Watching how comfortable Jada was with him pricked at Emily. Not only at how close they were but the fact that she could be so open about it.

"We need you, Ax," Jada's voice held genuine concern.

Emily reprimanded herself for not understanding their bond. Jada was married to another man, but she and Silas shared so much history, including the children they were trying to raise together. Silas had tried several times to explain it, but now Emily was seeing it first-hand.

Silas's eyes were shut now, but there was no way to know if he was awake or not.

"I didn't know Dad had tattoos." Will stared at Silas's arms, not fully covered by the hospital's thin fabric gown.

"Perhaps you should ask him about them someday," Emily said, a stab at Will for not visiting his *vater*. The boy wasn't her student anymore, but there were still things she could teach him. "Cover him up," she said, commandingly. "They're your *vater's* shame, and the others will be arriving soon." Natasha gently lifted Silas's arm and pulled the thin cover over him, Will doing the same on the opposite side.

A knock at the door sent all eyes that direction. A nurse entered, a heavyset woman, probably in her forties with hair pinned to the very top of her head. "I'm going to need to clear the room. We'll allow one or two of you at a time in here. The rest can go to the waiting room just down the hall."

Emily pressed her lips together. If she were his wife, she'd have a permanent place beside his bed, but as it was, she'd have to count on Silas's family to help watch over him. She took one last look at Silas, before following Will to the door.

72

She sat down on a soft couch next to a stack of magazines and prayed for Silas to recover, the knot in her stomach twisting tighter. She was supposed to be married today, only she hadn't shown up. What would Clem say?

About twenty minutes later, Natasha came to her and said, "You can go in now." The look in the girl's eyes broke her heart, but Emily hurried back to the room where Silas lay with his eyes closed, Jada beside him. She longed to hold him, and kiss his forehead, but that was impossible. As it was, she shouldn't even be here. Beholding the man before her, who had cared for her so many years, she was determined that he get well. Her life could never be the same without him.

"How long?" Jada asked quietly.

"What?" Emily still had her eyes on Silas, wondering if they'd ever pick strawberries together again.

"How long have you been in love with him?"

Emily's head snapped in Jada's direction, and all the blood ran out of her face. "Silas and I are just friends. Very *guete* friends." Her voice timid.

One side of Jada's mouth curled up along with an eyebrow. "Uh, huh. I figured it was a long time. And does he love you, too?" Her eyes narrowed.

Emily's mouth dropped open. "Silas took a vow before God when he married you. He won't break it." *Even though you did.*

"Natasha said you were supposed to be married

today."

Emily looked away. "It wasn't meant to be."

"Because you love Ax."

Emily gave her a pointed look. "I told you, we're just *guete* friends."

"Then why was he asking for *his* Emily?"

"He was?" Emily's eyes ran longingly over Silas's face, still covered by an oxygen mask.

"So now my only question is, why you were going to marry someone else." Jada stared a hole right through Emily.

Can she read my thoughts? Heat rose to Emily's face under Jada's scrutiny. She swallowed hard, and feeling the weight of her burning eyes, she broke out in a sweat. "Silas wanted me to marry Clem," she blurted out.

"Why?" Jada's eyes opened wide with surprise.

Emily remained silent, clenching her teeth.

Jada's words came out slow, and thoughtful, "Because they won't let Silas marry again, that's why. Wow, you must really hate *me*, then." Jada seemed more amused than accusing.

Emily ventured to look into Jada's eyes. She may as well tell her everything. "*Nay*, I pray for you daily, that you'll come to a faith in the Lord like Natasha and Silas have."

Jada's expression had dropped from her face, leaving her to stare blankly, but a sound from Silas sent all eyes to him.

"I'm here, Silas." Emily waited patiently for any indication that he was going to be all right. He mumbled something, the glazed look remaining, giving his dark eyes an almost wicked stare. Jada lifted the oxygen mask from him and pulled it down on his beard.

"I love you, Emily," he said weakly. Emily's heart swelled, and her cheeks boiled. He couldn't be saying these things in front of everyone, and he wouldn't be if he weren't so out of it. He needed her, and she hoped he wasn't trying to say goodbye forever. She couldn't let that happen.

She reached under the cover for his hand, no longer caring about her secret getting out to Jada. She gave her a tense glance and then drew closer to Silas's face. "Shhh, quiet love," she whispered, "someone will hear."

Silas took a deep breath and Jada replaced the mask.

Emily's heart pounded. Any moment the men of the community would be coming through the door and what would they discover?

"Please, Jada, don't let him say anything to the others. They'll shun us both, and we'll never live down the shame."

"What do you want me to do?" Her tone said she would comply.

"Stay in here with him, don't leave his side. And don't let him talk to anyone." Emily bent her head down to Silas's ear, hoping Jada wouldn't hear what she whispered. "I'll love you forever, Silas. Stay with me."

With Silas's eyes closed tight, Emily hurried back to the waiting room and sent Will in. She and

Natasha sat on the long couch together.

"God's going to take care of Daddy," she said. "I just know it."

Emily smiled at the young lady beside her, so full of faith. "We must pray hard." Not only for Silas's life, but that Jada wouldn't betray their secret to the bishop, the very one who shunned Jada years ago.

Emily fought the urge to run and hide when she saw the matching black felt hats approaching. Bishop Amos led the way, followed by John Miller, Leo Schwartz, and Emily's *beau*, Clem Wickey. Emily stood with shaking legs as they gathered around her.

"How is he?" the bishop asked.

"Not well, Bishop. He went into shock about the time the ambulance arrived. Now he's talking out of his head." She hoped that would give her a little insurance in case the unthinkable happened.

"I knew he was sick," Leo said, "but I didn't know it was that bad. He said he had a stomach bug."

"They think it's a virus from a tick bite. The antibiotics from the doctor didn't work." Emily glanced at Clem and back to Leo.

"May we see him?" Bishop Amos asked.

"Two at a time," Emily said, "but Jada's in there with him now. You can take turns." Emily wondered if they would decide not to go in at all, as being alone with Jada wasn't any more proper than Emily visiting with Silas alone, but about that time the group dispersed, leaving Emily and Natasha standing there with Clem.

"May I have a word with you?" Clem asked.

She nodded bravely. "I'll meet you outside."

This was a conversation she was dreading, however, getting it out of the way sounded rewarding enough that she was willing to do it. She turned to Natasha when Clem had gone.

"Are you going home with Clem?" The girl appeared anxious at the prospect.

"I've decided to call off the wedding, but I have no other way home."

"You can stay with us," she said excitedly.

"I don't know if your *mueter* would like that."

"We have plenty of room. I'm sure she won't mind. But if she does, we can take you home. Please? Daddy needs you. I need you."

Emily let out a tense breath. "Okay, but right now I need to talk with Clem."

With each step, Emily felt closer to her fate. It was both exciting and unnerving. She could never leave Silas, and it was a mistake to try. Clem's eyes were intense. She'd betrayed him, and knew she deserved his reprimand.

"I'm sorry, Emily," he said as they began walking down the endless maze of hallways.

He was sorry? "For what?"

"I didn't realize how sick Silas was. I know he's a friend of your family and I should have listened to you when you said to postpone the wedding. I promise to listen to you more in the future." His eyes were a soft blue, and tender as a hug. She was amazed at his compassion and forgiveness at her disobedience, but the pull was no longer there to stay. Emily had made up her mind to remain single forever, and love the only man she ever really had eyes for, even if it would always be from a distance. "Clem, I can't marry you. I'm sorry."

"What?" Clem's voice rose in surprise.

"Let me explain." She took a deep breath. "When you came into my life, I wanted a family of my own more than anything in the world. But now I realize, I already have one. God has given me all that I need to be happy in my students, and my friends, and my family, and if I marry you, and move out of the district, I'll lose all of that. I'm sorry it took so long for me to see it. Please forgive me, Clem."

He nodded slowly, coming to an understanding. "I'm sorry, too. I'll miss you, Emily." His complete lack of anger was almost a disappointment, but it was their way. Until the marriage ceremony was complete, a gal had full right to a *ja* or *nay*, and a broken promise was better than a lifetime of regret. She pictured what Silas would do if he were Clem. Never would he let her go so easily.

A lightness came over Emily now that her mind was made up and Clem had accepted it. "I'll miss you too, Clem." She would miss him, just as she'd miss her chance at children of her own, but she knew now she'd have missed Silas more.

As if rehearsed, the hallway had wound them in a circle and brought them back to the waiting room, its double doors opened wide. A knowing look passed between the two of them and Emily entered, leaving Clem behind.

It was up to Emily now, to see that Silas recovered. She took stock of the men in the room. The bishop and Leo were both missing, but Emily knew only one was supposed to go back at a time with Jada. She sat down on the couch and scanned the room until her eyes settled on a set of cushy chairs by the far wall. There Jada sat with Natasha. Emily jumped up and rushed over to them. "I thought you were going to stay in there."

"They asked to come in together so they could pray over him. I stayed until the nurse came in and repeated the rules, 'only two at a time.' Neither one of them budged so I had to leave."

"What's the big deal?" Natasha asked.

"Nothing," Emily and Jada said in unison, causing Natasha to lean away from them in her chair.

A tense moment passed.

"Mom said you could stay with us as long as you want."

Emily glanced at Jada for confirmation.

"You helped Natasha so much with her school work. I think she's even up for some scholarships. It's the least we can do."

"Danki," Emily said without thinking. "I mean, thank you. That's very kind of you both." Emily knew getting along with Jada would be much easier after today, and for that she was grateful.

"Did you get your wedding re-scheduled?" Natasha asked.

Emily bit her bottom lip. "We've decided to call it off. Clem's a good man, but I'm not ready to leave my home or my job at the school."

Jada's eyes flashed a knowing at Emily's bending of the truth, but it wasn't accusing. Had she been wrong about Jada all these years?

Just then, the bishop and Leo walked in and sat down. Emily had hoped they would leave. It was nice having so many people gather around when you needed them, but with the truth-telling medications Silas was on, the fewer people, the better.

The clock on the wall of the waiting room said ten. The large window showed the vast city of Springfield lit up under a full moon. Finally, the bishop stood and stretched his legs. Then, he stepped over to stand beside Emily. "We're going to go now, and let our driver rest for the night. Would you like a ride home?"

"*Nay, danki.* I'm going to stay with Jada and Natasha tonight."

"Jada is still shunned under the rules of the *Ordnung.*"

"I understand Bishop, but I'm a guest of Natasha's, and she needs me right now."

He hesitated, but only for a second. "Very well." He wrote out the names and numbers of a couple of drivers they used. "Call one of these men. They have wives that can accompany them when you need a ride home."

"*Danki*, Bishop."

Emily watched them leave and as soon as they were out of sight, she rushed to Silas's room. Will passed by as she entered, leaving her alone with Silas.

She sat down on the chair beside him and watched his chest slowly rise and fall for the next hour.

Soon, Jada poked her head in. "We're going home, are you ready?" Jada asked.

Emily fought back tears. "Don't you think someone should stay and watch him tonight, in case he needs anything?"

"Well, I've got a husband to get home to."

"I could do it if you can't. I'd be happy to." She blinked quickly.

Jada nodded.

"Will you be back in the morning?" She fought the urge to beg Jada to stay with her, knowing the night would be a lonely one, especially if the nurse kicked her out into the waiting room.

"Yeah, I'll be back about eight. Call me if anything happens."

"I will."

Jada gave her a long look, not hiding her pity, then turned to go.

"Thank you, Jada. For everything." Emily's voice was shaky.

Jada gave her a thin smile and then closed the door behind her.

Chapter 6

The next morning, Emily awoke to Jada hovering over her with a covered container. Startled, Emily's eyes ran over her, suddenly remembering the events of the previous day. If she weren't sitting beside Silas's bed in a hospital, she would have sworn it was some awful dream. Yet, if it hadn't been for Silas's illness she'd be Mrs. Clem Wickey this morning. She shook off the thought and received the container from Jada.

"What's this?"

"Oatmeal."

Emily tilted her head. "Organic?"

"How'd you know?"

Emily smiled as she took the lid off. Jada handed her a plastic bag with a spoon in it.

"Thank you."

"How'd it go last night?" she asked.

"No change. I think he slept all night."

"I meant how'd it go with you staying in the hospital all night?"

Emily found it strange that Jada was interested in her well-being, but she answered, "I dozed a little in the chair. I'm fine."

Just then, the doctor arrived, and practically ignoring both the women, he pulled on Silas's eyelids, flashing a light in them. Emily stood, setting the oatmeal on the chair. Then the doctor pulled back the covers, exposing Silas's legs. Emily turned her back as he reached for Silas's gown. A glance at Jada made her drop her head as well.

"Looks about the same," the man said.

Jada tapped Emily's arm. "What's wrong with him, Doctor?"

"We received his blood-work from the CDC. It's a rare tick-borne illness called Heartland Virus. There's no treatment for it." The man finally turned his attention to Jada and Emily.

"Is he going to die?" Jada asked.

"I don't know. All we can do is keep him comfortable, push fluids through him, and…" He shook his head, "wait it out." He gave them a solemn look before exiting.

Emily sat down with her oatmeal in her lap, stunned by the doctor's words, while Jada began pushing buttons on her phone. Emily couldn't stand *Englishers* because they were always looking at their phones instead of at the people talking to them. How could she do that at a time like this?

Jada squinted at her phone. "It says here there have only been a handful of cases of Heartland Virus. Two cases were farmers in Missouri, who spent weeks in the hospital before recovering. Here's another that was fatal. The disease spread to all his tissues." She sent a tense glance to Emily, slipping her phone back into her purse.

Emily couldn't stand to hear what might happen to her Silas. She needed to have faith. God had saved him for a reason. He would heal from this, and if it took weeks, she'd be right here with him the whole time.

It had been over a week since Silas had last spoken to anyone. Emily had returned from a few hours sleep at Jada's house and waited for the bishop and Leo Schwartz to go home for the night.

Emily had faith that Silas would be made well, but as each new day rolled around, it was beginning to grow thin. She sat down on the chair beside his bed with a tall foam cup of coffee on the table beside her. Never in her life had she liked the taste of coffee, but it helped her stay awake through the night as she waited for a miracle. If she rested her arm just right on the side of the bed, she could hold Silas's hand comfortably, but it was of the utmost importance that she didn't fall asleep that way and she found caffeine did the trick nicely.

It was difficult to get used to the dead-still feeling of Silas's hand, but talking to him helped. Not only did it pass the time, but she hoped it somehow let Silas know she was there, and would never leave him again. She chatted with him about everything she could think of and when she ran out of things, she'd start over and say them all again.

"How are you, Silas? Did you have lots of visitors today?" Emily waited, hoping he was forming a response in his head, if not with his mouth. "I've been thinking a lot today about how I've changed so much over the years and not all of it has been for the better." She reached for her coffee, and took a big sip, holding the warm cup close. "But you...you get sweeter, and kinder every day. I admire that about you. You always came to me when you thought your faith was weak, but you're the strong one." She'd made her peace with God about her actions, out on the road on the way to her wedding, telling Him she'd obey no matter what. The answer she received from God had led her here.

"I haven't always been honest, Silas. I've lied a lot over the years to you, and to God, but mostly to myself. I remember the day you made the first strawberry bed. I lied to the *Englisher* that came to the door. I told him you were my husband. I never told you I did that, but after the incident with Kenny, I can't stand *Englishers*. I know it's wrong. Do you think God will forgive me for that?"

A whoosh of air filling the bags around Silas's legs to prevent blood clots was the only answer.

"I lied to you when I said I'd never leave. I left you, Silas. And I shouldn't have. If I hadn't, you wouldn't be here right now."

She sighed heavily, the smell of bleach becoming more normal as each day passed. The machines beeped and the blood pressure cuff attached to Silas's arm started inflating. Emily waited patiently for the number and held her breath until it flashed on the screen: one hundred one over seventy-six, a good number. She glanced back to Silas's face, his eyes sealed shut, reminding her of the way she'd found *Dawdie* when he'd passed on in his sleep. She swallowed hard, looking away.

"I lied to God when I said I'd follow Him and followed after you instead. But this time, He led me here. I'm obeying God and He wants me here with you, to take care of you. To be your friend. You're my best friend, Silas, and I don't know what I'd ever do without you." Emily took a big drink of her coffee, feeling the caffeine running through her veins, hoping above all else Silas would know how much she cared for him.

"More times than I can remember, I lied to myself. Always thinking everything was okay. But it wasn't, Silas, and you knew. You always knew and kept telling me, but I didn't listen. *Dawdie* would have said it was my red-hair that kept me from it, but not you. You just kept loving me each day, hoping I'd finally see it for myself. And when I did, I was angry with you for it. But I had no right."

Cora, the night nurse, entered without knocking, giving Emily an empathetic smile. "How is he?"

Emily glanced at his face again, noticing the darkness under his eyes was worse than yesterday, but she'd never say so out loud. "Same."

Cora checked the numbers on the machine and touched the bag of fluids that was attached to a long tube leading into Silas's arm. "Just give us a beep if you need anything."

Emily smiled the best she could until the nurse was out the door and she and Silas were alone once again.

After a long silence, she said, "What we have isn't normal, Silas, I'll admit. But it's special, nonetheless. I'll accept it for what it is, and I hope you will, too. 'Cause I'm not leaving. Not ever. If you want to get rid of me, you'll have to leave, but I pray you won't. I'd spend the rest of my life missing you if you did."

Emily pulled the Bible from the side table drawer and read to him for a long while from Psalms, hoping it would cheer both of them. It didn't. She closed the book even more downcast than when she'd opened it, an unusual occurrence. She set it down beside her and began recounting the time Silas saw the bear in the yard. "I'll never forget the look on your face after I chased the bear away," Emily reminisced. "I had never been so afraid of losing you—until now."

Emily tried to keep her one-sided conversations with Silas upbeat, but it was getting more and more difficult. She glanced at Silas's face. It didn't even look like him anymore. "It feels like…" She stopped, wondering if she really wanted to finish her sentence and start crying again. "Like you're slipping away." The muscles in her face ached from crying so much. She had burst into tears every time she laid down to take a nap at Jada's and every morning in the restroom after spending another lonely night with Silas where he neither said a word nor moved. But she'd always tried to remain strong while in Silas's presence—until now.

The machine beeped and the blood pressure cuff inflated again, but Emily was too afraid to look at the numbers. What could she or the doctors do if they dropped down to nothing? There was no cure for this illness. It was up to God to heal him, and Emily didn't presume to know the mind of God.

"Come back to me, Silas," she cried. "Please come back." She laid her head on the rail of his bed and gasped to get enough air in her lungs. "Dear God, please bring him back."

Emily knew it was wrong to be so negative in her thinking. He would get better. She would have faith, and it would happen. It had to. She took hold of his hand again, and to lift her own spirits she began to sing. "Amazing grace, how sweet the sound, that saved a wretch like me." She raised her voice to keep herself from crying, not caring who heard her giving her faith a jump start. "I once was lost, but now am found, was blind, but now, I see." When she came to the next verse, Emily's faith was growing, her body felt purified and calmer. "Through many dangers, toils, and snares, I have already come, 'tis grace that brought me safe thus far, and grace will lead me home."

Danki, Lord, for Your peace. I know You saved him for a reason. May I be Your servant to fulfill Your work in him.

Just then, she felt a twitch in Silas's hand. She gasped. *Viel dank, my Lord. Thank You so much.* Emily squeezed Silas's hand with both of hers. "I'm here, Silas. It's me, your Emily." His face was still and when he didn't answer, Emily began singing the next verse, waiting patiently for another sign. "When we've been there, ten thousand years, bright shining as the sun, we've no less days, to sing God's praise, than when we first begun." Another twitch lit Emily with delight. She sang the song over and over again that night, hoping it would make a difference to both of them.

When morning came, Emily's faith was fully restored. She stood, knowing the others would soon be coming. She tucked Silas's hand under the blanket and kissed him on the forehead. "Goodnight, Silas," she whispered, knowing it was almost time for her to rest somewhere. His eyes fluttered open, almost halfway, and then closed again.

"Oh, Silas, I've missed you so much." She kissed his forehead again, and then both his eyes, cradling his head in her hands. They blinked again but looked too heavy to stay open. She placed her hand on his cheek, but a shuffling of feet drew Emily back.

Jada entered with Natasha, there to relieve her from her post.

"He's awake," Emily said, relief flooding.

"Did he say anything?" Natasha asked.

"*Nay*, he just opened his eyes a second ago." But they were closed solid now. It didn't matter. She'd seen it. Silas was getting better.

Emily refused to leave the hospital the rest of the day, wanting badly to receive word that Silas was up and about, but it didn't happen. When darkness descended, she hadn't slept at all in twenty-four hours. Settling in with her extra-tall coffee, Emily began chatting away, and somewhere in the wee hours of the morning, began telling Silas about how hurt she was when he'd kissed her goodbye.

"I lied to you, Silas. I had said yes to Clem, but I hadn't meant to. I just wanted to kiss him to see if it would help me forget about you. It didn't." She laughed softly. "Now I know nothing ever will."

Suddenly Silas's eyes blinked open and he said something. Emily strained to hear, glad the mask was reduced to tubing in and out of his nose.

"What is it, Silas?" She stood with a quick breath and hovered over him, her face close to his.

"Who's Clem?" he said in a weak voice.

Emily laughed with delight. "Welcome back," she said, brushing his hair behind his ears with her fingers.

"I know you," he said, his eyes floating around her.

"*Ja*, you'd better know who I am."

"Are you my wife?" he asked.

Her face fell. He wasn't joking. He'd been through a terrible ordeal and woke up confused. She'd give him a moment to straighten things out in his mind. "I'm Emily. Your…neighbor." What was she supposed to say she was to him? He wasn't her *beau*. It was…complicated.

"I remember you," he said slowly.

Relief washed over her. He remembered something. "What do you remember?"

"Watching you cook," he said.

"*Ja*, anything else?"

"I don't know."

Emily pushed the call button on the side of the bed, and a nurse's voice said, "Can I help you?"

"*Ja*, this is Ax Moreland's room." Emily had such a hard time with the nurses calling him Ax, she'd started using his real name when she spoke with them. "He's awake and he's having trouble remembering things." Her hand shook as she held the button down. "Could you send a doctor in?"

"I'll see what I can do."

She smiled at Silas, trying to put his mind at ease.

A long while later, the doctor stepped in. It was almost time for his morning rounds anyway. "I'm glad to see you're talking this morning," he said, shining a light in Silas's eyes. He took hold of his hands. "Squeeze as hard as you can."

The doctor glanced over at Emily and then back at Silas. "Can you tell me what year it is?"

Silas's face twisted and his breathing started to get harder.

"It's okay. That's normal. How about this question, "Who is this woman beside you?"

Silas peered over at Emily. "I can't remember her name right now. It's on the tip of my tongue."

"So you remember talking with her before today."

"Yes."

"Can you tell me your full name?"

Silas's eyes darted around. "It's either Silas or Ax?"

The doctor's eyes asked Emily to confirm.

"Ax Chase Moreland, but he changed it to Silas when he joined the Amish community."

"Silas, are you Amish?"

He thought about it a moment. "I don't know."

"Listen, Silas, you're having some issues with

your memory, but you're getting better and over the next few weeks you should show a lot of improvement. Hang in there, okay?" The doctor turned to go, but Emily stopped him before he reached the door.

"Why can't he remember anything?" she asked.

"We only have a few documented cases of this virus, and in two of them there were some memory issues. One cleared up in two weeks, the other took two years, but they both recovered fully."

"So he could be like this for years?"

"It's possible. Just try to keep him calm about it. He needs his rest."

Emily nodded, then returned to Silas. There wasn't much time before the others would arrive. "Silas, do you remember anything else about me?"

A faint grin grew on his face. "I think I remember your lips to mine."

Her heart stopped. "Silas, we're not married." She hoped to make him understand before she left him to babble their business to everyone who visited.

His face went blank. "Why wouldn't you marry me?"

"This is very important that you listen carefully and trust me. You're Amish now, but you weren't always. You aren't allowed to tell anyone who you're in love with. It's forbidden. Please keep those thoughts and memories a secret, for your own sake—and for mine." Her eyes held his and a seriousness passed between them.

Natasha entered. "He's awake!"

"*Ja*, come see your *vater*, Natasha." Emily motioned for Natasha to sit on the chair beside the bed.

"Listen, he's probably going to say some pretty strange things. He's a little…confused right now. Just tell him to rest, okay?" Emily waited for Natasha to nod an understanding before she said a quick goodbye to Silas and hurried to the waiting room to find Jada.

Emily sat down beside her at the table by the window. "He's awake, but his memory isn't good."

"Like amnesia?"

"The doctor said one of the patients with Heartland Virus had memory issues for two years, but eventually he recovered."

"Poor Ax," she said. "Well, at least he's talking now."

Emily nodded. No one else was in the waiting room at the time, and Emily was beat. She rested her head on her propped up hand on the table. Now she would worry all day that Silas would reveal their secret to everyone.

Jada handed her a lidded bowl.

"What's this?"

"It's a mixture of chickpeas, alfalfa sprouts, cucumber, onion, green onion, fresh corn, and authentic Mexican salsa." Jada smiled with satisfaction at the dish she'd prepared.

"Thank you." Emily opened it and poked a chickpea with her fork. As crazy as Jada's diet sounded, it didn't taste half bad.

"I need you to keep an eye on him today. He's remembering pieces of things, but I'm afraid he may let more slip than he intends to. Would you do that for me?"

Jada sipped her cup of coffee. She nodded in agreement. "So you two are...intimate."

"Nay," Emily said quickly, setting her fork down. "We would never go against God in that way. He made a vow before the Lord."

"Yeah, but you didn't."

"It would make me an adulteress—which I'm not." She picked her fork back up, but couldn't bring herself to eat.

"Wow."

"What?"

Jada shrugged her shoulders. "Well, you're young and pretty. I've just never pictured Ax with so much...restraint."

Emily's eyes couldn't meet Jada's anymore. "It's usually Silas who reminds me," she said lowly.

Jada laughed a little. "Even more surprising. I figured Ax would have moved out of the community a long time ago."

"Why must you call him Ax?" Emily asked. This woman knew her darkest secret, she supposed they were past pleasant formalities.

"He'll always be Ax to me."

"He changed his name when he moved into the community because he wanted the world to know he wasn't the same man he was before. God transformed his heart and his mind. He's a whole new person. When you call him Ax, it only throws his past sins in his face."

"I guess I always saw it as a game he was playing, trying to pretend he was someone else when he

94

wasn't."

Emily stirred the chickpea salad with her fork. "Huh, for a while there I thought you knew him better than me, but you don't. He's trying his best to do right by you and the children because he's a good man—a changed man. He's only close to me because you left. I would never interfere with his relationship with you just like he promised never to interfere with me and Clem."

"What happened with Clem, anyway?"

Emily paused a moment, gathering her thoughts. "I can't make marriage vows I can't keep. As hard as I've tried not to, I love Silas, and always will."

"So you're just going to stay single forever?" Jada shrugged her shoulders, shaking her head in disbelief.

"What choice do I have?"

Natasha walked in with concerned eyes. "Daddy's talking crazy. Will one of you come in with me?"

They both stood and Emily carried her bowl with her to Silas's room. All three of them stood against the wall, allowing a nurse to walk through. It wasn't the same nurse as usual, and no one made the suggestion that one should leave so that only two would be in the room.

Jada stood close to him. "Hi…Silas. How are you?"

"I remember you," he said, his eyes squinted.

"I'm Jada, your ex-wife."

"*Ex*-wife?"

"Right," she said. "And you remember Natasha, our daughter?"

"I have a daughter, but she's younger than that." Silas's eyes were still far away, apparently lost somewhere out there with his mind.

"Nope, this is her. She's just growing up fast."

Emily admired the calm way Jada spoke to Silas, laying out the facts for him, but not making a big deal out of not remembering whole family members.

"Do you feel like talking with us a bit?" she asked.

"What about?" He had an almost child-like innocence about him.

"Anything you want to tell us about."

Emily began to squirm, crossing her arms in front of her to keep herself still. She didn't want him talking about just anything.

"I remember fighting a bear. A big, scary bear," he said. "He had me on the ground and I thought I was dead."

Natasha flashed worried eyes at her *mueter*. "He's out of his head, Mom, what do we do?" she whispered.

"*Nay*, that really happened." Emily watched as Silas's eyes lit up. "I was in the garden and you told me to go to the house. I went inside and the bear attacked you. Do you remember what happened next?"

He thought a second. "You saved my life."

"I did," she whispered with a faint smile.

"How?" Natasha asked.

"Ask your *vater*."

"How did she save your life, Dad?"

"She brought out my pistol and shot at him till he ran away." The way Silas said it made her sound brave.

"Do you remember the time I broke my arm?" Natasha asked. "And you came and helped us at our house?"

Silas thought a second. "I remember driving you to school, but I don't remember you breaking your arm. How did that happen?"

Natasha explained the wreck they'd had. They spent an hour or more with Silas just going over memories to see what he could remember. He seemed to enjoy it and had most of the major events down. Most importantly, it brought Natasha closer to her *vater*, learning things about him she didn't know. Emily smiled, feeling strangely like a real part of Silas's family.

Silas stepped out of Jada's car on shaky legs. It had been a week since he started trying to remember everything and he hoped he was close to having all his memories back, but how could one really be sure of something they'd forgotten? With Jada on one side of him and Emily on the other, he made it inside to the bed. He lay down there, determined to give himself a few days to recover and then he was going back to work. It wasn't fun lying around all the time, and Silas was tired of people waiting on him.

He gazed up wearily at Jada and Emily, the only two women he ever really loved, wondering how on earth they'd came together for his sake. But that was the kind of women they were—caring.

"Well, I guess you can take it from here," Jada said to Emily.

"Thank you for all your help, Jada. I don't know what I would have done without you."

"You're the one who put in all the long hours."

"Well, you drove me around the last two weeks and gave me a place to stay, and meals, too."

Silas smiled wearily up at them from his bed. "Are you two going to fight?" He laughed. It felt good to laugh again. The last time he lay in this bed, he thought they'd carry him straight to a hole in the ground. "Thank you both, for taking care of me. I don't know what I've done to deserve either one of you in my life."

They each smiled at him and planted a kiss on his forehead before leaving the room. He couldn't believe that, either. Emily had told Jada their secret. How that came about, he'd probably never know. But one thing he was sure of, God had a hand in everything that had happened. He didn't know how, but he trusted God would work it all out for good.

Silas took a little nap and when he awoke Emily was sitting at the side of his bed with a plate of food for him. He never thought he'd see that happen again, either. She was supposed to marry Clem. He sat up and Emily adjusted his pillows for him.

"Are you comfy now?" she asked.

"Yes. Thank you."

Her pretty face set his heart at ease.

"*Guete*. Leo just left. He did your chores today, and now that we're alone, I was hoping we could have a little chat about what you remember."

He laughed, noticing her eyes were bluer than ever. "I could never forget you, Emily."

Her eyebrows slanted downward. "Are you sure?"

He held out his hand and with a curious look she held hers out, too. He pulled her close to him on the bed in a warm embrace with her by his side. He whispered in her ear, "I remember the night we hid from Clem in your room. You fell asleep in my arms and I held you till morning. I didn't sleep a wink, though. And I remember one winter when the ice storm came and I followed you in the kitchen and—"

"Okay," Emily said, pulling away and standing up. She fiddled with the strings on her *kapp*. "I think you're recovering your memory quite well." She cleared her throat. "Well, good night, Silas. I'll bring your breakfast in the morning." With shy eyes she walked out the door, leaving him there with a plate of food.

He certainly was glad she hadn't married Clement, and with the way she did it, he doubted if any man in the community would ever ask her out again. And while he felt bad for her, he understood. He didn't think he could ever marry another, either. *Thank you, God, for my Emily. She may never be my wife, but she'll always be my friend. Bless her richly, Lord.*

Chapter 7

Emily sat down between Jada and Natasha in the long row of folding chairs set up on the football field. On the other side of Natasha, Silas sat looking for Will in the sea of blue hats and robes. "Is that him?" he asked Natasha.

"I think so," she said.

Jada crossed her legs toward Emily. "I can't believe my babies are all grown up. It makes me feel so old."

"You're not that old."

"Says the girl still in her thirties."

"You're only forty-two," Emily said. "And you eat healthy. Your skin looks younger than mine."

"You're just saying that." Jada had divorced again, making her very unhappy with herself, and she didn't know it had nothing to do with her looks.

Emily laughed. "I used to be afraid of getting old, now I just embrace it."

"If I were thirty-five, I would, too."

Emily and Silas had both tried to convince her that there was still forgiveness in the Lord if she just repented of her ways and chose to believe in God, but as much as she liked to complain about getting older, it seemed she gave no thought to the life beyond this one.

"Oh, they're starting." Jada sat up straight in her chair, peering over the crowd.

"When will he come through?" Emily asked.

"It's alphabetical so somewhere in the middle."

Emily peeked around Natasha at Silas. They weren't allowed to sit together in public, but getting together with Silas's children and even Jada, made Emily feel almost like she and Silas were a normal couple. They had stopped fighting their fate and decided to take their relationship for what it was. It wasn't wrong to love each other, only to act upon it. So after Silas recovered from his near-death illness, Emily had stopped holding his hand each day and there were no more sweet kisses to the forehead. He'd kissed her hand once, when he thanked her for saving his life. But now, all they were left with were kind words—some rather flirty—spoken in hushed whispers throughout the day, and often an I love you before they each retired to their homes for the evening. They had unspoken vows to love, protect, and care for each other till death parted them.

And that was how their secret had stayed hidden all these years from everyone except Jada, who wasn't telling, seemingly more fascinated with it than anything.

Emily turned her attention to Natasha, a grown woman now, in college to become a teacher. She sat in a long dress with a soft flower pattern, her hair in a bun. She'd been attending the local Mennonite church in Asheville but hadn't joined yet.

Will had spent more time with Silas on the farm, but now was leaving for college, too. As they said Will's name, everyone cheered, and Emily prayed that he would find work close, staying in touch with Silas, and accept the Lord into his heart before it was too late.

After the graduation was over, Jada invited them

both to go with them to Wheezie's to eat, but Silas refused. Emily could tell he didn't want to be rude, but Jada was still shunned, and it wouldn't do for the community to see them eating at the same table with a shunned person.

It was evening when they returned to the farm. Emily brought Silas his supper on the front porch, and they watched the sun go down and the first fireflies of the year appear. "I can't believe another summer is almost here already. You don't usually see this many fireflies for at least another month." They sat a while longer before she said, "There's something relaxing about fireflies. They help me sleep."

"You know what helps me sleep? Chocolate lava cake."

Emily's mouth opened in a smile. "How did you know I made a cake for dessert?"

"I saw you making it through the window this morning." He grinned mischievously.

"Silas Moreland, I'd say you were a peeping Tom." She knew Silas was all over the property doing chores during warm weather and it was very likely he happened by the window when she made the cake that morning before they left for the graduation.

"I thought that was only if I watched you through the bedroom window."

She turned her nose up as she said, "Well, you'd best stay away from *all* my windows."

"I haven't peeked in your bedroom in quite a while," he teased.

She laughed and went inside for two pieces of cake. When she returned, he was sitting on the porch swing, in the spot next to where she always sat. She handed him his cake and carefully sat down. It wasn't like Silas to sit that close, but no one was around, and she could sense he had been on edge for most of the day. Emily took a bite of her cake. Then, looking at it, she asked, "Are you okay, Silas?"

"Yeah," he said. "I'm just not in any hurry to go home tonight."

They ate their cake in silence, then Emily set the dishes on the porch rail and sat back down beside him. She pressed her lips together. "Do you want to talk about it?"

He sighed. "I did my best, you know? And both of them are doing fine. In college, out on their own. They even have scholarships and I'm so glad for them."

"But you wish they were here with you."

He caught her eye. "Is that selfish?"

"*Nay*, when you think about it, all we really have in this life is each other. Nothing else is more important than being with the ones we love."

He turned to Emily, his face becoming even more serious. "Will you still sit with me on this porch, when we're old and gray?"

Often Emily had wanted to ask Silas the same thing, but decided it was far too sappy for Silas to want to discuss. She leaned back and let her foot rock the swing just enough that it creaked. "*Ja*, I'd like that very much."

The glimmer in his eyes told her he had been comforted by those words.

They sat a long while in silence before retiring to their own homes for the night. A few hours later, after Emily took her hair down and put on her nightgown, she blew out the lantern, but a light still shone in the room. On the windowsill was a jar full of fireflies. As she picked up the jar, she felt the love he had given her in the deed. He must be feeling what Emily did when Natasha left. Emily took the jar outside on the front porch to release them, and there sat Silas on the swing. "I knew you wouldn't keep them overnight." He smiled.

She opened the jar and set it on the porch floor in front of the swing, then sat down with Silas. He took her hand in his, something they never did, and then covered it with his other hand. The warmth spread all over Emily, but she knew he was trying to comfort himself. She rested her head on his shoulder and they watched each little light fly away into the dark sky.

It had been two weeks since the graduation, and Silas was still holding Emily's hand on the porch at night after dark. She liked the attention but was beginning to worry about him. He had said he just needed to feel closer to her. Emily prayed hard that God would comfort Silas in all the ways she couldn't.

It was evening, and a cool rain beat down. Emily knew Silas would never come inside the house for supper without someone else present, and didn't want to push things since he'd probably change his mind about holding her hand any day now. So she made him a plate and covered it with plastic wrap. Running in Silas's kitchen door without knocking, she found Silas staring at her.

"You didn't have to go out in the rain. I was going to come and get it."

She knew he was telling the truth, but she'd been going out of her way to do nice things for him since he brought her the fireflies. "Your supper," she said, handing it to him.

"Danki," he said, catching her eye. He hadn't studied her that way in a while, and she knew it meant trouble was coming. If it continued, he'd work his way up to hugging her, or kissing her, or something inappropriate, and he'd regret it. Emily couldn't let that happen. "I'd better go," she said.

"I miss talking with you over supper."

She did, too. "The rain won't last forever, and I'm free the rest of the summer. Plenty of time for suppers on the porch."

He gazed into her eyes with unbridled longing, sending Emily's heart into an erratic rhythm.

A knock at the door stopped her heart completely. With a jump, she bolted for his bedroom and shut the door behind her. No one could see her alone with Silas in his house, especially this late in the evening. She just prayed the visitor wasn't looking for her. Just in case, she slipped into Silas's closet and shut the door. She heard a voice, but couldn't understand a word of it. The closet door flung open, and Silas pressed his finger up to his lips. He spoke in the lightest whisper. "It's Will. Jada's sick and she's asking for me."

"Go with him. If you're not back by morning, I'll get someone to do your chores and hire a driver to come see her myself."

With worried eyes, Silas looked Emily up and down. She could tell he didn't want to leave, but she wasn't sure if it was because he wanted to be on the place to protect her at night, or because of the heavy feelings of loneliness he'd been experiencing lately.

She placed her hand on his cheek. "I'll pray for you both," Emily said. "Now go."

He took a raincoat from the closet and pulled down his black felt hat from the shelf above her head, and out the door he went, leaving Emily alone in Silas's house, his supper untouched.

The next morning after breakfast, Emily walked outside to hitch the buggy when a car pulled up the drive. The rain had stopped finally, leaving a cool, clean scent in the air. Emily hurried back inside and watched through the kitchen window as Silas stepped out of the car. When the car had gone, she ran outside to meet him, but by this time he was inside his house. She knocked before entering. "Silas, are you okay?"

"Emily," he said urgently, as if he were looking for her. He grabbed her by the elbow and pulled her to sit down at his kitchen table, but he remained standing.

Then he shook his head, pulling his beard and pacing.

"What happened? How's Jada?"

"I…" He shook his head again.

"Sit down, Silas, you're making me nervous."

He sat on the chair beside her, but pulled it closer to stare intensely into her eyes.

"Start at the beginning," she said.

"Natasha had taken Jada to the hospital when Will came to get me. Jada was passing blood, and very ill. That's why she sent for me. She said I was the most religious person she knew and she wanted me to pray for her."

These words, along with the stunned look on Silas's face made Emily shake in her very core. What's happened to Jada?

"I told her God wanted to talk to her alone. That she had to ask God for forgiveness, truly believing He sent His Son, Jesus, to die for her sins, and ask Him to save her."

"Did she?"

Silas's face was blank. "Yes. And then she died."

"Jada's dead?" The shock of it brought Emily's hands flying to her mouth. "What happened to her?"

"They don't know. She had been feeling tired a few days, then got a fever and was nauseous, but didn't go to the hospital until the bleeding started. They gave her fluids and ran some tests, but she died before they even got the results."

"Natasha," Emily whispered. "Is she okay? I need to go to her. Is she at home?"

"I'm supposed to meet with her and Will later

today to get funeral arrangements out of the way. I told her she could come home with me for the rest of the summer if she wanted. Will has a job lined up for before his first college semester starts and he's going to stay close to school in an apartment with some friends."

This was all so sudden. Emily just couldn't believe it. "I sat next to her at Will's graduation only two weeks ago. Now she's gone?" Emily shook her head in disbelief.

Suddenly she realized the full impact of the situation. Her eyes grew wide as they darted around the room. "Jada's gone." Suddenly her eyes met his. "Oh, Silas," she whispered, her heart thumping in her ears. Did he realize what this meant? A knowing flashed in his eyes, and though it wasn't said, she knew he had had the thought, too.

The next few days were a flurry of mixed emotions. Jada had been Emily's friend, and all the time she'd spent praying for her had paid off, for she had found the Lord before she died. Emily imagined God welcoming her in with open arms, and the thought brought her heart joy. But Natasha and Will were left without their *mueter*, and while Silas handled everything well, and it brought them all together as a family, Emily couldn't help but think about poor Natasha, and how awful she must feel losing her *mueter* so suddenly.

When the funeral was over, Emily helped Natasha pack a few bags and together they headed to the farm. It was almost strange to see Natasha driving a car in a plain dress, like the two didn't belong together. But Emily supposed if she didn't want to become Amish, being Mennonite was the next best thing, and it was nice to have a woman driver for a change, rather than a man who was forced to bring his wife along to make the whole situation appropriate.

In the yard, Silas was waiting for them as they stepped out of the car. He took the bags from the trunk and started to carry them in. "Daddy, wait," she said, turning to Emily. "Would you mind if I stayed in your house with you a little while?"

Emily looked to Silas for reassurance but found little. "Sure, honey. Whatever makes you more comfortable."

Emily frowned at Silas. She knew he was hurting too, having loved Jada in his own way, despite everything she had done to him, and he wanted to spend all the time he could with his children. Emily hugged Natasha as Silas carried the bags into Emily's house.

Some of the community members had brought over food, knowing Silas had planned on gathering with his grieving children today, but Natasha wanted to cook.

"There's more than enough food here, what are we missing?" Emily asked.

"I just don't want to sit. At home, I would cook whenever I was nervous about something, and I remember all the good times you and I had cooking together." Natasha began to cry.

"Oh, honey. I know you miss her. I missed my *mawmie* like that, too. That's why I never wanted to leave this house. I have so many memories of cooking with her right in this very kitchen."

"I believe she's in Heaven, Miss Emily. I really do." Natasha hadn't called her Miss Emily in years.

"And you should be very glad in your heart about that."

Natasha sniffled.

"So what are we cooking today?"

"I know it sounds stupid," she said with a little voice, "but could we make alphabet biscuits?" She smiled through her tears.

"Alphabet biscuits it is," Emily said. She started pulling out pans from the cabinet as Silas and Will walked in. "Give us about twenty minutes and we'll have food on the table," Emily said.

Silas observed the flour sitting on the counter. "Are you cooking more food?"

"Mmm, not exactly," she said. "Just a little baking therapy."

By supper the next day, Will had gone back to finish moving into his new apartment, and Natasha was still working off her feelings in the kitchen. Silas tilted his head in an indication he'd like to see Emily outside—alone.

"I'll be back in a bit, Natasha," she said as she

slipped out the kitchen door.

"Will you go on a walk with me?" he asked.

She nodded, and they started across the yard. Not one word had been spoken about it, though they both knew what the other was thinking.

"How long?" he asked quietly, his hands in his trouser pockets as he walked.

"It's hard to say. I've never seen a situation like this one. I'd say the biggest concern is Natasha."

"Natasha loves you. You're already a part of our family."

"*Ja*, but she's devastated over losing her *mueter*, and she's clinging to me for comfort. I don't want to appear to be insensitive, for her sake."

"You're right. And we don't want the community thinking we were waiting around for such a thing to happen."

They stopped walking when they were a comfortable distance from the house. "Natasha will go back to school in the fall. What about then?"

Silas's eyes dropped down to Emily's lips. "Agreed, but it's going to be difficult to stay away from you. All this time there was no possibility of you ever being mine." The look of desire was back in his eyes, stronger than ever, sending feverish waves through Emily.

She lowered her voice even more. "I've been yours for a long time, Silas." She knew she needed to keep cool, not only for Silas's sake, but for Natasha's. She smiled at him playfully. "We'd better get back. Supper's almost ready." He brushed her hand with his as they began walking toward the house, leaving Emily to wonder if it were an accident or on purpose.

Chapter 8

It was three weeks before they had a cause of death for Jada—food poisoning.

"I don't understand it," Silas said from Emily's table. "Jada was one of the healthiest people I've ever known. Not an ounce overweight, she always ate fresh, organic foods, she even exercised."

Natasha sat across from Emily at the table. "They said it was organic spinach tainted with E. coli. There's a big recall now. It came from an organic farm out of state."

"Jada and I studied a lot about that when we decided to get into farming. You can't let the runoff from the livestock get into the vegetables. But what I don't understand is, why couldn't her body fight something like that off? I thought the worst cases were the elderly and young children," he said.

Emily couldn't understand it, either. The whole thing was so ironic, but she tried to stay out of the conversation, afraid of somehow sounding insensitive.

"Years ago, Mom started having some stomach issues and had her blood checked. It showed she had a mild intolerance to gluten."

"I remember her quitting all wheat," Silas said, pointing at her with his fork.

"After that, she started rotating her foods so she wouldn't become sensitive to anything else. So she would skip days for things like spinach. One day she'd eat it all day, and then she'd skip a day or two. If she had a whole bag of spinach, she probably finished it off by herself in one day before she even started having symptoms."

"So she overdosed on poisoned food." Silas's face showed understanding now. He shook his head and took another bite from his plate.

Natasha picked at her food with her fork. "Kind of makes you afraid to eat at all."

"Emily and I grew everything on your plate, Sweetie. Don't you worry."

Emily threw a tense look at Silas. "What he means is, God takes care of us and works things out in His own way. It was awful how your *mueter* died, but what if it had been suddenly, like in a car accident, never giving her the chance to make her peace with God?"

"She's right," Silas said. "And we know that all things work together for good to them that love God. We've all been praying for your mother for many years, so I'd call it an answered prayer, wouldn't you?"

"I guess you're right," Natasha said. "But it doesn't change the fact that I miss her."

"You will," Emily said. "But you can't mope around here forever. She wouldn't want that." She took a bite of a biscuit shaped like a letter 'Q'.

Silas shifted in his chair. "You also need to decide what you're going to do with your mom's house. You could sell it and live here if you wanted. Did she owe anything on it?"

"No. She got the house free and clear in the divorce settlement, and he got everything else."

Emily wondered what else could have been left. The house was huge.

"Sell it, and split the money with your brother. Then you can live here."

"Or rent an apartment," Natasha said carefully.

"What would your Mennonite friends say about it?" Silas knew they shared the same values as the Amish community. Emily smiled at his attempt to let his daughter come up with the correct answer on her own.

"They'd say I shouldn't live alone."

"Exactly."

"So I'll find some friends who want to split an apartment with me."

Silas rolled his eyes. "As long as you know you can trust them, they're all female, and you're not alone, I guess I'm good with it."

Natasha smiled for the first time that Emily could remember. It seemed Natasha was finally beginning to heal.

After dinner, Silas announced he was going to pick strawberries for a while for tomorrow's open market.

Emily's heart skipped a beat at the thought of him leaving. It hadn't been a common reaction for years now, but as she awakened to the idea of marrying Silas, those feelings of young love had begun to stir. "I can help you, as soon as I get the dishes done." She made silent eyes at Silas as Natasha gathered plates from the table.

"I can clean this up if you want to go on," Natasha said, not looking up.

Emily smiled knowingly at Silas. "That would be nice, Natasha, are you sure?"

"I need to stay busy," Natasha said. "I can come help with the strawberries, too, in just a bit."

"Very well. We'll see you out there." Emily strode out the door after Silas and with baskets in hand, they walked to the strawberry patch, not far from the house.

Silas laughed when they were out of earshot of the kitchen. "Something tells me I'm going to have more help today, but fewer strawberries to sell tomorrow."

"Would you rather me go back to the kitchen?" she asked.

"Oh no, now you're just teasing me." He grabbed her free hand.

"It's daytime, Silas, someone could see us."

"And what of it? I'm a free man; you're a beautiful, eligible woman." He brought her hand up to his chest and held it there.

"What about Natasha?" she asked.

"She'd have to be in your bedroom to see us from the house."

Still, it made Emily nervous. She pulled him along toward the strawberry patch.

"How much longer do we need to wait?" he asked.

Her breath caught at the mere question. "I'd hoped we could tell her right before she left."

He kissed her hand, holding his gaze on hers. "And now?"

She melted at his warm touch. "We just need to

wait for the right moment."

That evening when Silas came home after supper and Bible devotions with Emily and Natasha, he took off his shirt and boots and crawled into bed. Curling up with his pillow he inhaled the scent of Heaven.

Honeysuckle. He sniffed his bed all around to find the source, but only his pillow had the unmistakable smell of Emily's signature scent. The woman was toying with him, and he was enjoying it. Perhaps it was time for him to step it up a notch as well.

Emily wandered out to the barn, knowing good and well where Silas was. She told Natasha she needed to find a small piece of wood to level her sewing table, leaving the girl to make yet another batch of biscuits for today's dinner. Emily felt almost guilty helping her with the cooking, knowing it did her so much good to stay busy in the kitchen.

But Emily's mind wouldn't rest until she saw Silas alone. He was now her secret *beau*, and while she hated waiting to get married, she was thoroughly enjoying their flirtatious behavior. Yesterday, she'd put two drops of honeysuckle essential oil on his pillow, knowing he'd think of her all night if she did.

She snuck up behind him and wrapped her arms around his waist. He turned around without a word, took her hand to his chest, and leaned down to kiss her.

Emily shied away. "I don't kiss until the time of engagement," she said playfully. His eyes never changed from the determined look he had. He grabbed her hip, drawing her closer and took her mouth with his. She melted in his embrace. "Marry me," he said, kissing her again, his mouth moving over hers the way she'd always dreamed. When he finally released her she drew in a cool breath, cleansing her from the intense heat he'd just lit in her.

"I...think it's time to tell Natasha," she whispered breathily.

He nodded, giving her one more intense look she thought would be the end of her before he turned away and went back to work.

A light-headed Emily staggered out of the barn, trying to compose herself as she walked the distance to the house. It was almost July, a little over a month before Natasha was to go back to school, but it was apparent that if she didn't tell Natasha, she may well find out on her own by Emily's blushing. Or if she were anything like her *mueter*, she would see right through Emily, anyway.

"Natasha," Emily said when she came inside the kitchen. "I need to ask you something." Emily sat down in Silas's chair and waited for Natasha to come sit with her.

How could she put this? "Your *vater* has asked to court me, and I wanted to ask your permission first."

Natasha's eyes swelled. Then, a half-smile formed on her face. "You and Dad, dating?"

Emily cracked a tense smile, then nodded.

"The old dog. But why are you asking me?"

"I know you're having a hard time right now, and I didn't want you to feel like he was leaving you out. He's really missed having you around."

She gave a downward smile, "Well, don't let me stand in your way." Her almost comical eyes locked with Emily's.

"Is there something wrong with me courting your *vater*?"

"No. I just always thought of him as being too old to ever marry again."

Emily laughed. "Well, I think your *vater* has a lot more life left in him than you think."

It had taken four months for Emily and Silas to not only plan a wedding but start going out in public together. It had been very difficult at first. The impulse to hide and lie was so strong in Emily, she wondered if she'd ever be able to break the habit. "I'll make an honest woman out of you yet," Silas had said, laughing. But Emily wondered if she'd ever be fully comfortable.

Even riding in the buggy together was a new experience. She hadn't sat in the same buggy with Silas since *Dawdie* died. Now she stood over *Dawdie* and *Mawmie's* graves, the unmarked grassy spot where they rested, wishing they were here to see her marry today. It had been thirteen years since she'd spoken to her *vater* last, and nearly all of that time she'd spent loving a forbidden man. She hoped God had a long marriage planned for her and Silas, and that it would be as happy as her parents' was.

It was like starting a brand new life at the age of thirty-five. She'd already quit her job at the school, and no longer had to bite her tongue when the women at frolics talked about their husbands. She and Silas were allowed to go on outings into town, go on picnics, ride to church together, and sit beside each other when they ate at gatherings. She no longer feared shunning if she wrote a letter to him and it was found, or if someone caught them staring at each other across the room. They were free to love each other completely, or they would be, by dinnertime today.

"Are you ready?" Silas asked.

She took his outstretched hand and they walked through the cemetery to the buggy. He brought her around to her side and helped her up. It was an amazing feeling to be treated like a lady by the man she loved. All those years she'd traveled back and forth to work alone, in the storms, and even snow, but now she would stay home and help Silas run the farm, growing babies and organic tomatoes.

Silas sat down beside her and clicked his cheek for the horse to get moving. Down the road they went, waving to the plain folks they saw along the way, like Silas's good friend, Leo Schwartz and his wife, Beth. Emily's face flushed when she thought of how differently things could have turned out, had she married someone else.

The wedding was a small, private affair at Emily's sister's house. Natasha and Will were there and so were all of Emily's brothers and sisters.

Everything was cleaned up by dark and just like that, Emily and Silas were headed home as husband and wife. As the buggy rumbled down the road, the strangest feeling swirled inside Emily.

"What is it?" Silas said, peering over at her.

"Nothing. I just feel like we've committed a crime and someone will be coming to stop us any minute."

"You know, I thought the very same thing. I even glanced over my shoulder once or twice."

"Was anyone there?" she teased.

He stopped the buggy and turned to look. "Nope. Just me and my wife."

"Then kiss me."

His eyes flashed a wild look as his lips neared. Taking Silas's hat off his head, Emily ran her fingers through his hair, gently, her mouth in sync with his. Overcome with emotion, she pulled away.

"What's wrong?" he asked.

"I just love you so much, Silas," she said, tears of joy threatening, her wedding still feeling like a dream she was afraid to wake up from.

He pulled her into a tight hug. "I'm never letting you go, Emily. Not as long as I live. We'll grow old on your front porch swing, and watch our children chase fireflies in the yard."

"And pick strawberries together as a family?" she said with a broken voice.

He pulled back to look into her eyes. "And pick strawberries as a family. I'm so glad you waited for me. You're a wise, and faithful woman."

How awful it would have been had she married Clem after all. She wondered at God and His mighty plans. What would have become of them had she not given her will over fully to the Lord?

Emily wiped her eyes on her dress sleeve. "What are neighbors for?"

Epilogue

"Silas Moreland, you get down here this minute," Emily yelled.

Silas peeked around the corner of the house at Emily and their son playing by the mimosa tree in the yard. "Did you holler for me?" he asked.

"Nay," she said, a bit exasperated, her face glowing and her belly protruding.

Silas walked over to where they were and shot a look at his son, Silas, that had him jumping to get out of the tree.

"Dawdie," he said when he reached the ground. "How did you and *Mawmie* meet?"

"Ask your *mueter*," Silas said, surprised at the question.

"She said it was complicated and I should ask you."

Silas glanced at Emily, who was trying to hide a smile behind one hand. She was still as beautiful as she ever was. Fair skin, clear blue eyes, and long dark-red hair he only saw at bedtime.

"Oh, she did, did she?" He held out his hand for Emily. He squeezed it gently, an indication he needed help explaining things.

"Why don't you ask *Dawdie* to tell you the story about the bear, instead."

"A bear? Tell me, *Dawdie*. I want to hear."

They walked inside the kitchen, the yeasty smell of bread baking in the oven never failed to bring him comfort. Silas took his son up in his lap while Emily started supper. "One day *Mawmie* and I were working outside when out of nowhere a big black bear ran out of the woods and attacked me."

The boy gasped. "What did you do?"

"Well, I fought the bear with everything I had."

"And then what?"

Silas wasn't ashamed to say Emily had saved his life. It wasn't the first time, and may not be the last. "Your *mueter* ran out of the house shooting my pistol like a wild woman and chased the bear all the way into the next county."

"Really?" His eyes were wide.

"Something like that," Silas said, resting one arm on the table.

He exchanged smiles with Emily.

"Is he fibbin'?" the boy asked his mother.

Emily stirred the flour mixture in a large bowl. "Your *vater* was brave to fight the bear."

"I was scared out of my mind," Silas muttered.

Just then, Natasha breezed through the kitchen door.

Little Silas asked, "Natasha, did *Dawdie* tell you

the story about the bear?"

Natasha's face lit up. "I heard he punched him right in the mouth." She faked a punch in the air.

He turned back to his father. "*Dawdie*, if you were so scared, why did you do it?"

"To save your *mawmie*."

The boy laughed and pointed. "But she saved you. That's funny."

Silas often wondered which one of them had saved the other more. Perhaps when his son was older, and the situation permitted, he'd tell him about the other times.

"Did you have a good day at school?" Emily asked Natasha.

"Yes, but I have a huge stack of papers to grade tonight." Natasha was living in Silas's old house, engaged to marry a Mennonite man from Asheville. Silas would rather she stayed in the community, but somehow her *fiancé* had convinced Will to try the Mennonite church as well, and for that he respected the man greatly. Silas had given Natasha his old house, hoping she'd want to live there even after she was married.

"I have time for a game of kickball, though. Do you know anyone who would want to play?" she asked her little brother.

"I do, I do," he said, jumping up and running for the door.

"Watch for bears," Silas hollered after him with a half-smile.

Silas watched Emily at the stove for a long moment before standing and walking up behind her, gently wrapping his arms around her big belly. He let out a sigh by her ear, comforted by her nearness.

She turned around to face him, tucking her head beneath his chin. "You're a good *vater*, Silas. Do I tell you that enough?"

"Almost every day." He pulled back, directing her chin upward with his finger. "You're a good wife, do I kiss you enough?"

She smiled at him, her eyes taking on the dreamy state they always did when he threatened to kiss her. "Maybe once more, for good measure."

He kissed her gently at first, and then more, hoping that even though he wasn't a young man anymore, he'd still be able to make her dizzy. He released her and watched her eyes open.

"Silas," she whispered in sweet reprimand, patting him on the chest and taking a step away. "It's not even dark yet." Her blue eyes, playful and bright.

He couldn't wait to hold her tonight, especially when he remembered all the years he'd longed to hold her and thought he'd never have the chance. The pain of the long winters away from her still fresh in his mind.

She tilted her head to the side. "Are you okay?" she whispered, concern for him edging her voice.

He held out his arms once more, realizing his smile had faded. She hugged him gently, while he savored the smell of honeysuckle, one hand holding her *kapp*. "I am now."

If you enjoyed this series please consider telling a friend about it or leaving a review on Amazon.com.

Thank you for reading. God bless!

More Amish Fiction by Tattie Maggard

The Amish of Swan Creek
Book 1 (Sweet Competition)
Book 2 (Redeeming Ruth)
Book 3 (Abigail's Letters)
Book 4 (The Long Way Home)
(Also available in one money-saving paperback.)

A Swiss Amish Christmas
Book 1 (I Hear Christmas)
Book 2 (A Christmas Courtship)
Book 3 (The Christmas Stranger)

Coming Soon:
An Amish Rumspringa
Book 1 (What Happens in Asheville)
Book 2 (Stays In Asheville)
Book 3 (Finding Love in Asheville)

Made in the USA
San Bernardino, CA
13 January 2018